Corporate Protocol

Alex Mercer, Volume 1

adrian borowski

Published by DreamLand Books, 2024.

This is a work of fiction. Similarities to real people, places, or events are entirely coincidental.

CORPORATE PROTOCOL

First edition. October 21, 2024.

Copyright © 2024 adrian borowski.

ISBN: 979-8227176370

Written by adrian borowski.

To my Mother Barbara Borowska

Corporate Protocol
Alex Mercer Series Book 1
Written by Adrian Borowski

Introduction

There's a moment when you realize your life will never be the same. For most people, that moment comes quietly—an unexpected word, a look that lasts too long, a missed call that leaves a bad feeling in your gut. For Alex Mercer, it started with numbers.

Sitting at his desk on the thirty-second floor of a glass tower that stretched toward the sky, he was just a data analyst. The kind of person whose world was built around spreadsheets, algorithms, and the meticulous art of seeing patterns where others saw chaos. But on that particular morning, the numbers didn't add up.

It was subtle, almost imperceptible at first. A few transactions that didn't quite match, a shift in the figures that seemed too perfect to be real. Most would have ignored it, brushed it off as a rounding error or a glitch in the system. But Alex had learned to trust his instincts. And something about those numbers set off alarm bells in his head.

That was the moment, the moment everything started to unravel.

At first, he couldn't put his finger on it, couldn't see the full picture. But the deeper he dug, the more the pieces began to fall into place. And what he found was far more dangerous than he ever imagined.

The corporation he had dedicated his life to wasn't just skimming profits or hiding a few unsavoury business practices. It was something much darker, something that reached into the highest echelons of power. The company wasn't just a well-oiled machine, it was a front. A web of deceit, corruption, and greed that stretched farther than Alex could have ever believed.

He had stumbled onto a secret that wasn't meant to be uncovered. And in that moment, as the weight of the truth settled in his chest, he knew that he had crossed an invisible line.

There was no going back.

In the days that followed, Alex would learn what it meant to be hunted. What it meant to be on the wrong side of a billion-dollar empire, one that would stop at nothing to protect its secrets. He wasn't ready for the betrayal, the violence, or the loss that awaited him. But he had made his choice. And once you've seen the truth, there's no unseeing it.

This wasn't just about the numbers anymore. It was about survival.

Alex had uncovered something that had the power to destroy lives and now, his own life was on the line. The corporation's dark underworld was coming for him, and if he didn't act fast, he would disappear like the others who had tried to stand in its way.

As he stood on the edge of a storm that would tear his world apart, one question haunted him: How far was he willing to go to expose the truth? And how much was he willing to lose?

Chapter 1

The Discovery

The familiar hum of machinery echoed through the sleek halls of TitanTech as Alex Mercer walked through the automated doors of the colossal skyscraper, his eyes still foggy with the remnants of sleep. Every day at precisely 6:45 AM, the building's immense windows gleamed in the early morning light, casting shadows across the streets below. The city was alive, but TitanTech, the heart of the tech world, was in its own league—its employee's mere cogs in a vast, unfeeling machine that never stopped.

Alex blended into the crowd of sharply dressed professionals, though his faded grey jacket and jeans, comfortable yet understated, set him apart from the suits marching with precision around him. Most of them were ambitious executives or ambitious engineers gunning for a spot closer to Marcus Kane, the corporation's enigmatic CEO. Alex, though talented, had no such ambitions. He preferred numbers, not politics. The code didn't lie. It couldn't manipulate or betray.

He passed through security, nodding at Carl, the aging guard who waved him through without so much as a glance at his ID badge. Alex didn't miss the small, tired smile Carl gave him, a gesture of mutual understanding. Carl had worked here for over a decade, but to the other employees, he was invisible—just another fixture in the sprawling complex of glass, chrome, and secrets. That was TitanTech in a nutshell: glamorous on the surface, but indifferent to the lives it employed.

Alex made his way through the labyrinthine hallways to the data analysis department, a space as sterile and cold as the algorithms they processed. He stepped into his cubicle and sat in front of his triple-monitor setup, each screen flickering to life with streams of data and complex financial models. It was a symphony of numbers, and to Alex, it was beautiful.

Today, though, something felt different. There was an underlying tension in the air—a restlessness that buzzed beneath the surface of TitanTech's usual order. Maybe it was just him, but the usual office banter felt forced, the casual greetings among coworkers strained. He shook off the feeling, turning his attention to the data waiting on his screen. **Ignore the noise, Mercer. Focus on what matters.**

As he settled into his rhythm, his fingers dancing across the keyboard, Alex began combing through a seemingly routine audit. TitanTech ran dozens of subsidiary companies, and part of his job was tracking the financial health of each one. He was used to small anomalies—incorrect entries, human error. But today, there was something off in the patterns. A few wire transfers didn't match up. The sums weren't small, either—millions of dollars funnelled into accounts that shouldn't exist.

Alex leaned forward, squinting at the screen. He'd seen suspicious transactions before, but this was different. The transfers were methodical, meticulously hidden under layers of legitimate transactions. To anyone else, they might seem like just another blip in the system. But Alex's instincts, honed from years of analyzing data, told him otherwise. He ran a trace on the transactions, following the digital breadcrumbs as they wove through shell corporations, overseas accounts, and finally into an untraceable offshore entity.

A knot formed in his stomach as the trail led him to a name—**Kane Global Holdings**. He froze. Kane Global was Marcus Kane's private investment firm. It was common knowledge that Kane dabbled in various investments outside TitanTech, but nothing about these transactions felt above board.

He reran the analysis, hoping it was an error, a misplaced number, or a misfiled report. But each time, the result was the same. Alex felt the hairs on the back of his neck stand on end. He had uncovered something much larger than a simple accounting mistake.

"Mercer, you're about to burn a hole through that screen," came a voice from behind.

Startled, Alex turned to see Lena Thompson leaning casually against the doorframe of his cubicle. Her purple-dyed hair contrasted sharply against the sterile office environment, her tattoos peeking out from the sleeves of her hoodie. Lena was TitanTech's cyber security specialist, and one of the few people in the company Alex genuinely trusted. Their friendship had grown over years of shared projects, mutual respect, and late-night brainstorming sessions.

"You're going to love this one," Alex said, his voice low, gesturing for her to come closer.

Lena raised an eyebrow, pushing off the doorframe and moving to stand beside him. She scanned the screen, her sharp eyes narrowing as she took in the details. "Jesus, Alex… what the hell is this?"

"That's what I'm trying to figure out. It looks like someone's laundering money through Kane's private investment firm. Big money."

Lena let out a low whistle. "If Kane's involved, you're looking at more than just financial fraud. This could be a whole damn empire."

"Exactly," Alex said, his fingers running nervously through his hair. "But we can't just take this to HR or legal. If this is tied to Kane, then it's above their pay grade."

"You're right about that." Lena leaned in closer, her face inches from the screen. "We need more than just this. We need evidence—proof that this isn't just a few rogue transfers."

Alex's heart pounded in his chest. He had known uncovering corruption in a corporation as vast as TitanTech would be dangerous, but this felt like standing at the edge of an abyss. One wrong move and they would both fall.

"Okay," he said, his voice steadying. "We dig deeper. Quietly."

Lena straightened and crossed her arms, her expression serious. "And you're sure about this? Once we start pulling at this thread, there's no going back. If Kane finds out you're digging into his business…"

Alex met her gaze, his jaw tight. "I know the risks. But I can't let this slide. Not when there's so much at stake."

Lena was silent for a moment before giving a slow nod. "Alright, Mercer. But we're gonna do this smart. No rushing in blind. We take our time, gather every piece of data we can, and then we move."

Alex nodded in agreement, though the weight of what they were about to do pressed heavily on his chest. "Thanks, Lena."

"Don't thank me yet. Let's hope we're both alive when this is over."

By the time the sun had set, the day's events still churned in Alex's mind. He sat in his small, cluttered apartment, the only light coming from his laptop screen. The world outside his window was still, the city's constant hum a faint background noise. He had spent the last few hours cross-referencing more data, confirming his earlier suspicions. Every click of the mouse was a step deeper into the labyrinth.

Suddenly, his phone buzzed, vibrating across the coffee table. He glanced down at the screen, expecting a message from Lena or a routine notification.

Alex frowned and unlocked his phone.

STOP DIGGING. THIS IS YOUR ONLY WARNING.

The message was short and direct, but the effect was immediate. His pulse quickened, his throat tightening. How did they know? He had been careful, hadn't he? Panic gripped him for a moment as he looked around his apartment. Were they watching him? Had someone hacked his phone or his computer?

The rational part of his mind told him to calm down, to think. But the primal part of him—the part that knew when danger was near—was screaming at him to run. He stood up, pacing the room, trying to collect his thoughts.

Whoever sent the message knew he had found something. Which meant they were close. Too close. His instincts told him to delete everything, to erase every trace of his investigation and pretend this day had never happened. But another part of him, the part that couldn't stand injustice, told him to push forward. To expose whoever was behind this, no matter the cost.

He grabbed his phone, dialling Lena's number.

"We have a problem," he said the moment she answered.

"Tell me."

"I just got a message. Someone knows I've been looking into this."

There was a pause on the other end of the line, and when Lena spoke again; her voice was calm but firm. "We need to move fast. Don't do anything rash. I'll be there in fifteen."

The line went dead, and Alex felt the tension in his chest tighten. He walked over to the window, peering down at the street below. Cars moved lazily through the city, pedestrians walked without a care in the world. But he knew better. Somewhere out there, in the shadows, someone was watching. And they wouldn't stop until they had silenced him.

When Lena arrived, her eyes were sharp and focused, any hint of their usual playful banter replaced by a cold determination. She didn't waste time. "Let's see your computer."

Alex sat down; pulling up the encrypted files he'd been working on. Lena leaned over, her fingers flying across the keyboard as she checked for traces of intrusion, her eyes flicking between windows as if she were chasing invisible ghosts through cyberspace. "No breaches," she said finally. "They didn't get in through your system. They're watching you from the outside."

Alex clenched his fists, frustration and fear battling within him. "What do we do now?"

"We go dark," Lena said simply. "We take this offline. No more digital trails. From here on out, we work in the shadows. If we're going to bring them down, we'll do it the old-fashioned way."

Alex nodded, feeling the weight of the decision settle over him. There was no turning back now. He had crossed a line, and there was no erasing what he knew. The only option was to see this through to the end, whatever that end might be.

As they prepared to leave the apartment, Alex glanced one last time at his phone, the warning still glaring up at him from the screen.

He wasn't just fighting for his life anymore. He was fighting for the truth. And the truth would be their greatest weapon.

Chapter 2

Into the Shadows

The drive to Lena's apartment was tense. The city lights blurred by as Alex stared out the window, his mind racing with possibilities, and each one darker than the last. He was no stranger to data—numbers, code, algorithms—those were his world, things he could manipulate and control. But this? This was different. This was real life, and real life wasn't bound by the neat, clean logic of data sets. People lied. People killed.

Every street they passed seemed to have a set of eyes watching him, lurking in the dark corners. Was someone tailing them? Every black sedan or white van felt suspicious. Lena, driving with one hand on the wheel and the other on her phone, her eyes flicking up to the rear-view mirror every few seconds, clearly shared his paranoia.

She broke the silence first. "You need to keep your head straight, Alex. If you let the fear get to you, you'll make mistakes."

"I know," Alex muttered, his gaze still fixed outside. "It's just—"

"I get it," she interrupted, her voice more sympathetic now. "This is different. But we can handle this. We're not amateurs."

Alex took a deep breath, forcing himself to focus. Lena was right. He wasn't helpless. They had the skills and the knowledge to dig deeper, find out what exactly Kane was hiding, and most importantly, how to protect themselves while they did it.

As they pulled into the underground parking lot of Lena's apartment building, Alex felt the tension in his chest ease slightly. This was familiar territory—Lena's safe house of sorts. She had taken extra precautions when it came to security, knowing her line of work often required discretion. The building itself was nothing special: a concrete, brutalist structure built in the 80s, one of those places that blended into the cityscape without drawing attention.

But inside Lena's apartment, things were different. The moment they stepped through the door, it felt like entering a tech bunker. Monitors lined the walls, servers hummed softly in a corner, and encryption equipment was scattered across the desk like a mad scientist's lab. Every window was covered with thick blackout curtains, and the only source of light was the glow of LEDs from the machines.

"Welcome to the nerve center," Lena said with a wry smile as she tossed her keys onto the counter.

"I forgot how cozy it is in here," Alex replied, half-joking as he took in the dimly lit room.

"We've got work to do," Lena said, snapping back into focus. "Let's break down what we know and what we don't."

Alex took a seat on a worn leather chair near her desk as she powered up her main terminal. A cascade of screens flickered to life, each displaying different streams of data, system diagnostics, and real-time network traffic. For all its chaos, this was Lena's kingdom—and here, she was queen.

Lena began tracing the breadcrumbs from Alex's initial findings. "You said the wire transfers all point back to Kane Global Holdings, right? I'll cross-reference that with known shell companies tied to Kane and see if we can find a pattern."

Alex leaned forward, his elbows resting on his knees as he watched her work. "There were a few offshore accounts I couldn't trace—too many layers of obfuscation. It felt deliberate."

Lena's fingers flew over the keyboard. "Of course it's deliberate. Kane didn't get to where he is by leaving trails. He's had years to perfect the art of misdirection." She paused as new windows popped open on her screen, showing lines of transactions, some dating back over a decade. "Look at this. These accounts aren't just laundering money—they're buying influence. Politicians, government contracts, even foreign dignitaries."

Alex felt a chill run down his spine. "How far does this go?"

Lena looked up from the screen, her face serious. "Far enough to make people disappear."

Her words hung in the air like a threat, a reminder that they were now tangled in something far more dangerous than they'd imagined.

"I need more time to dig," Lena said, her eyes flicking back to the screen. "We need to be sure before we make a move. You should go home, get some rest."

Alex shook his head. "I'm not going anywhere. I need to see this through."

Lena sighed, clearly not surprised by his stubbornness. "Alright, but if we're going to stay here, we're doing this right." She pulled a battered duffel bag from under her desk and began pulling out burner phones, encrypted USB drives, and a small stack of cash. "We're going dark. No more phones, no more internet, except through these." She tossed Alex one of the phones. "This is our new lifeline."

Alex caught it and examined the cheap, disposable device. "You've really thought this through."

"It's what I do," Lena said, her voice dry but with an edge of pride. "Now, let's see what other skeletons we can dig up on Kane."

They spent the next few hours poring over data, their focus sharp as they followed trails, cross-referenced transactions, and slowly pieced together the bigger picture. Kane Global Holdings wasn't just laundering money—it was acting as a middleman for all kinds of illegal activities: weapons deals, political bribes, corporate espionage. And the deeper they went, the more it became clear that Marcus Kane wasn't just another corrupt CEO—he was a kingpin.

It was well past midnight when they finally paused, their eyes bleary from staring at the screen for so long. Lena stretched, rubbing the back of her neck. "We've got enough to make some noise, but not enough to take him down. We need something concrete. A smoking gun."

Alex leaned back in his chair, exhaustion settling in. "What if we don't find it in time? What if they come after us before we can finish this?"

Lena's face hardened. "That's why we need to be smart. Kane has resources—people on his payroll who'll do anything to protect him. We're playing a dangerous game, Alex, and the stakes are our lives."

Alex ran a hand through his hair, the weight of the situation pressing down on him. He hadn't expected things to escalate this quickly. What had started as a routine audit had now turned into a full-blown conspiracy, one that could end with him and Lena dead if they weren't careful.

As if reading his thoughts, Lena added, "We'll stay one step ahead. But you need to be prepared for the worst. Kane's not the kind of man who forgives, and once he realizes you're a threat, he'll come at you with everything he's got."

The words hung between them like a death sentence.

Suddenly, there was a soft knock at the door.

Alex's heart skipped a beat. He glanced at Lena, who was already on her feet, moving silently toward the door. She motioned for him to stay put as she reached into a drawer and pulled out a small handgun, her movements precise and fluid.

The knock came again, louder this time.

Lena pressed herself against the wall beside the door, her finger resting on the trigger. She met Alex's gaze, her expression cold and focused. Whoever was on the other side of that door wasn't a friend.

In the silence that followed, Alex could hear his own heartbeat thudding in his ears.

Lena held up three fingers, silently counting down. Three... two... one.

In a flash, she yanked the door open, gun raised. But instead of an attacker, a man in a brown delivery uniform stood on the threshold, blinking in surprise.

"I-I have a package for Lena Thompson?" he stammered, holding out a small box.

Lena lowered the gun, her body still tense as she grabbed the package. "Thanks," she said curtly, not bothering to apologize for the gun pointed in his face.

The deliveryman mumbled something under his breath and hurried down the hallway, leaving them alone again.

Lena shut the door and set the box on the counter, her eyes narrowing as she examined it. There was no return address. Just her name in bold black letters.

Alex stood, moving closer to get a look. "What is it?"

Lena opened the package carefully, as if expecting it to explode. Inside was a small, black USB drive.

"Who sent this?" Alex asked, his voice tense.

Lena didn't answer right away. She plugged the drive into her laptop, her fingers hovering over the keyboard as she waited for the contents to load.

A single file appeared on the screen, labeled: **For Your Eyes Only**.

Lena clicked on it, her eyes scanning the document. As she read, her face paled.

"What is it?" Alex asked, his heart racing.

She looked up at him, her voice barely above a whisper. "It's everything. All the proof we need. The whole operation."

Alex stared at her, trying to process what she was saying. "Where did it come from?"

"I don't know," Lena replied, her voice shaky. "But whoever sent this—they know more than we do."

Suddenly, the gravity of their situation hit Alex full force. They weren't just playing a dangerous game—they were pawns in someone else's.

And the question that now loomed over them wasn't whether they could take down Marcus Kane.

It was whether they could survive long enough to try.

Chapter 3

Closing In

The sun had barely begun to rise when Alex opened his eyes. He felt more drained than rested, his body aching from the tension of the previous night. He sat up slowly, the weight of everything that had happened the day before pressing heavily on his chest. The USB drive, the package, and the faceless figure who had sent it. He couldn't shake the feeling that he and Lena were now standing on the precipice of something far bigger—and far more dangerous—than either of them had anticipated.

Across the room, Lena was already awake, seated at her cluttered desk, her face illuminated by the glow of multiple monitors. She hadn't slept. Her posture was rigid, and the dark circles under her eyes hinted at her exhaustion, but her focus was unbroken. Alex watched her for a moment, admiring her ability to drown out the chaos around them and zero in on the task at hand. The tension in the room felt palpable, as if the very air were coiled, waiting for the next strike.

"You need to rest, Lena," Alex said, his voice soft as he stood and stretched.

Lena didn't look away from the screen. "No time for that. Whoever sent this drive knows more than we do, and if we don't figure out who they are soon, we're screwed."

She clicked rapidly through more files, her eyes scanning rows of text and encrypted messages. Alex could hear the soft hum of servers and the occasional tap of keys in the otherwise silent room. He walked over to her desk, glancing at the data flashing across her screens. The familiar names of companies, shell accounts, and offshore holdings blurred before his eyes. But one name stood out among them, glowing like a warning beacon—**Marcus Kane**.

Alex clenched his fists as he read through the documents. Each folder revealed more about the shadowy operations Kane had been orchestrating behind the scenes. Shell corporations, anonymous accounts, weapons smuggling, political payoffs,Kane was at the center of it all.

Lena's voice broke the silence. "These aren't just random deals, Alex. This is a carefully constructed web. Kane has been building this empire for years, slowly and quietly. He's got people everywhere, politicians, military contractors, foreign governments."

Alex's stomach turned. The magnitude of what they had uncovered was staggering. "How is this even possible? How has no one exposed him?"

Lena's fingers paused over the keyboard. She turned to Alex, her expression hard. "Because the people who get too close either disappear or end up on his payroll. The ones who resist? They don't last long."

Alex took a deep breath, the reality of their situation sinking in. "We're not just dealing with corporate corruption. This is something much bigger."

"Yeah," Lena said grimly. "We're talking global crimes. Arms deals, illegal surveillance, human trafficking. Kane's got his fingers in all of it."

The enormity of what they had uncovered was like a weight pressing down on Alex's chest. They had stepped into the lion's den, and the lion was far more dangerous than either of them had realized.

Lena clicked on a folder labeled **Black Falcon**. Inside were documents, photographs, and several video files. They watched in silence as the videos played, each one showing a clandestine meeting between shadowy figures, briefcases exchanged, hands shaken. Men in military uniforms, foreign officials, and business tycoons—all captured in dimly lit, grainy footage. But there was one constant figure in each of the videos: Marcus Kane.

"He's orchestrating everything," Lena whispered, her voice thick with disbelief. "These are international deals. Weapons sales. Bribery. He's using TitanTech as a front for a global crime syndicate."

Alex felt cold as he watched Kane's calm, commanding presence in each video. The man had crafted an empire of deceit, and he had done it with a ruthless efficiency that left no room for doubt. Every move was calculated, every deal carefully negotiated.

"This is the proof we need," Alex said, his voice hardening. "We take this to the authorities, and he's finished."

Lena shook her head. "It's not that simple, Alex. Kane's got people in law enforcement, too. We can't just waltz into the nearest police station and hand them this. We need to be smart about how we use it."

Alex slumped into a chair, the enormity of the situation weighing heavily on him. He was out of his depth. This wasn't the world of data analytics and financial projections. This was the world of shadows, a place where people like Kane thrived—and where people like Alex got crushed.

But he couldn't walk away. Not now.

The sudden buzz of Alex's phone shattered the tense silence. He reached for it, frowning as he glanced at the screen. **Unknown Number**.

He felt a knot form in his stomach. His first instinct was to ignore it. Lena, who was now standing behind him, looked at the phone suspiciously. "Don't answer that. It could be them."

Alex hesitated. Could it be Kane? Or worse, someone else who had been monitoring their every move?

But something in his gut told him to answer. He swiped to accept the call and put it on speaker.

"Alex Mercer," said a deep, gravelly voice. The tone was calm, almost bored, but there was a menace beneath it, like the growl of a predator sizing up its prey.

Alex's pulse quickened. "Who is this?"

"Who I am doesn't matter," the voice replied smoothly. "What matters is that you've made a grave mistake."

Lena's hand shot to the keyboard, immediately beginning to trace the call, but the voice continued unfazed. "You and your little hacker friend have been poking around in places you don't belong. That USB drive you're so fond of? Consider it your last warning."

Alex's hands gripped the edge of the desk. "Who are you working for?"

A soft chuckle. "You think you're in control here? You think this is a game where you have all the pieces in place? Let me be clear, Alex—you're nothing. Less than nothing. Kane will destroy you. And if you're smart, you'll hand over what you found and disappear."

Alex's heart raced, anger bubbling up beneath the fear. "Why should I believe you?"

The voice hardened. "Because if you don't, the people you care about will suffer. You might think you're clever, but you're not untouchable. Neither is your friend."

The call cut out abruptly, leaving a heavy silence in the room.

Lena looked up from her screen, her expression grim. "Whoever that was, they're good. No trace. It's like they never even called."

Alex sat back in his chair, his mind spinning. The faceless caller's words echoed in his head: *the people you care about will suffer*. He glanced at Lena, who was already working on tracing the files again, her brow furrowed in concentration. She was part of this now, whether she liked it or not. And whoever was behind this knew exactly how to get to him.

"We need to get out of here," Alex said, standing abruptly. "We've been compromised."

Lena's eyes flicked up to him. "Out of here? Where?"

"They're watching us. Whoever that was, they know we're digging. They know too much. We can't stay here."

Lena nodded slowly, understanding the gravity of what he was saying. "We'll go underground. I've got safe houses. But we need to move fast."

Alex grabbed his jacket, his mind racing with possibilities. Whoever had called him had made it clear—they weren't safe. They were being hunted. And the only way to stay ahead of the predator was to disappear entirely.

Lena moved quickly, gathering her most critical gear: burner phones, encrypted hard drives, laptops, and enough cash to get them through a few weeks off the grid. She handed Alex a burner phone and a small, nondescript bag. "Only take the essentials," she said briskly. "We don't know how long we'll be underground."

"What about the data?" Alex asked, his voice tight with anxiety. "We can't just leave it behind."

"We won't," Lena assured him. "I've got backups, encrypted and stored in places even Kane can't reach. But we need to move now. If they're watching, they could be on their way."

The two moved quickly, working in sync as they packed up their essentials. Lena's apartment, with its dense array of tech and surveillance gear, suddenly felt like a deathtrap. Every window, every wall seemed to hide a pair of eyes, watching, waiting.

As they finished packing, Lena paused, her face paling slightly. "Alex... what about your family?"

Alex froze. His family. The thought hadn't even crossed his mind in the whirlwind of the last few hours. His sister lived across town, and his parents were retired, living peacefully in a small house outside the city. He hadn't spoken to them in days, too wrapped up in the chaos of the investigation. And now... they were at risk.

"They could use them to get to you," Lena continued, her voice low. "We need to make sure they're safe."

Alex's mind raced. What if they were already being watched? What if Kane's people had already targeted them? The thought made his stomach churn.

"We need to go to them," Alex said firmly, grabbing his keys.

Lena shook her head. "No, we can't go directly. If they're watching us, we'll lead them right to your family."

"Then what do we do?" Alex demanded, panic creeping into his voice. He couldn't let anything happen to his family—not because of him.

Lena thought for a moment, then grabbed one of the burner phones. "We'll contact them. Tell them to get out of town, somewhere remote. But they can't know why. The less they know, the safer they'll be."

Alex nodded, trying to keep his breathing steady. Lena was right. They needed to protect his family without drawing attention to them. But the fear gnawed at him, a cold knot in his gut. He wasn't just fighting for his life anymore—he was fighting for theirs too.

Lena quickly dialled the number for Alex's sister, keeping the conversation short and cryptic. She told her to take the family on a sudden vacation, anywhere outside the city, for "security reasons." It was enough to raise concern but not alarm. Alex prayed it would be enough.

As they finished packing, Alex's mind was already racing ahead to the next steps. They would go underground, disappear from the grid, and continue their investigation in the shadows. But the threats had become very real. They weren't just up against Kane anymore—they were up against an entire network of power and corruption that would stop at nothing to silence them.

Lena grabbed her bag and slung it over her shoulder. "Let's go. The longer we wait, the closer they get."

With one final glance around the apartment, Alex followed her out the door. The game had changed. Now, it wasn't just about exposing the truth.

It was about staying alive.

Chapter 4

Under the Radar

The city streets blurred past as Alex gripped the wheel of the old, inconspicuous sedan Lena had arranged for their escape. The car, a beat-up navy-blue sedan with no discernible features, was the perfect getaway vehicle—anonymous, forgettable, and blending seamlessly into the background of the city's morning rush. Lena sat beside him, her sharp eyes scanning every vehicle they passed, every pedestrian that came too close, her mind clearly working a mile a minute.

Alex's knuckles whitened as he clenched the steering wheel, his eyes darting between the road ahead and the rear-view mirror. Every dark car they passed made his pulse spike, every flash of a figure on the sidewalk sent a bolt of anxiety through his chest. He had never felt like this—like prey. And yet, with every turn they took, it became clearer that someone, somewhere, was hunting them.

"They'll be looking for patterns," Lena said, her voice tight as she stared out the window. "We need to avoid the highways and stay away from any spots with surveillance cameras. Stick to back roads and alleys as much as possible."

Alex nodded, but his mind was racing with thoughts of his family. He had spoken to his sister, Maria, only briefly, telling her to pack up the family and leave town for a while. It had been difficult to keep the panic out of his voice, but she had agreed, though confused by the suddenness of it. He didn't have time to explain, and the less she knew, the safer they would be.

"They'll be safe, Alex," Lena said, as if reading his mind. "You did the right thing. They're out of the city by now, and they're not on anyone's radar. Our focus needs to be on keeping us off the grid."

The words were meant to comfort him, but Alex couldn't shake the fear that had taken root deep inside him. His family had no idea what was really happening, how deep this conspiracy went, and how ruthless the people behind it were. And if Kane's network wanted him, they'd stop at nothing to use his family as leverage.

"We'll get through this," Lena continued, her eyes still scanning the road. "But we need to stay ahead of them. They'll have people on the lookout. We're not dealing with just a corporation here, Alex. This is a global operation with resources far beyond what we can imagine."

Alex gritted his teeth. "Then why don't we just disappear? Get out of the country, go someplace they can't reach us?"

Lena shook her head. "You can't run from people like this. They'll find you. They always do. The only way to survive is to outsmart them."

"And how do we do that?" Alex asked, frustration seeping into his voice. "How do we stay one step ahead when we're up against people who control everything?"

Lena's expression hardened. "We know something they don't. We have the proof of their operation, and that's our leverage. As long as we have it, we have some control."

"Some control?" Alex scoffed. "They've already threatened us, and we're on the run. How much control do we really have?"

"We have enough to make them afraid," Lena said, her voice icy. "And fear makes people sloppy."

Alex didn't respond, but Lena's words sank in. They had proof, hard evidence of Kane's illegal operations. That meant they had power, but it also made them a target. They were in a dangerous game, one where the rules weren't clear, and the stakes were life and death. The only way out was to play smarter than the people chasing them.

The car crept through the narrow back streets of the industrial district, far from the gleaming skyscrapers of TitanTech's headquarters. Here, the roads were rough, lined with dilapidated warehouses and abandoned factories. The kind of place where people disappeared without anyone asking questions.

Lena had chosen this route deliberately. It was the part of the city where no one paid attention. There were no security cameras, no foot traffic, no reason for anyone to care about two people driving in an old sedan.

They pulled up to a rundown building with boarded-up windows and graffiti covering the walls. It looked like it hadn't been used in years, but Lena knew better. This was one of her safe houses, a place she had prepared for situations just like this.

"Come on," Lena said, grabbing her bag from the backseat and stepping out of the car. "We'll be safe here for now."

Alex followed her inside, the air thick with dust and the smell of mildew. The interior was just as grim as the outside—a dim, concrete room with bare walls, a single table, and a few chairs. But it was secure, with reinforced doors and windows, and most importantly, it was off the grid. No one would be able to find them here.

Lena set up her laptop on the table, connecting it to a secure network she had built over the years. Alex marvelled at her preparedness. This wasn't just a safe house; it was a command center, equipped with encrypted communications, multiple layers of firewalls, and enough tech to stay hidden from anyone trying to track them.

"How many of these places do you have?" Alex asked, setting down his bag and taking a seat.

"Enough," Lena replied cryptically. "I've been in this game longer than you think. I know how to stay invisible when I need to."

She tapped a few keys on her laptop, bringing up a map of the city and surrounding areas. "We need to start laying low for a while. I've got burner phones, fake IDs, cash, everything we'll need to survive off the grid. But we can't just hide forever. We need to find out who sent us that package, and why."

Alex leaned forward, his heart pounding. "Do you think it was someone on the inside? Someone working with Kane?"

"Could be," Lena said, her fingers flying over the keyboard. "But I don't think so. Whoever sent that package wanted us to have it. They didn't just stumble onto this. They knew exactly what they were doing."

"What if they're playing us?" Alex asked, his mind racing. "What if this is all a setup?"

Lena paused, considering the possibility. "It's crossed my mind. But if they wanted us dead, they could have sent a hit squad instead of a USB drive. No, whoever sent this wants something from us."

"Or they want to use us to take Kane down," Alex said. "We're the perfect scapegoats."

Lena shrugged. "Maybe. But right now, we don't have a choice. We need to play along until we figure out who's behind this."

Alex stared at the map on the screen, the realization dawning on him. This wasn't just a fight for survival anymore. They were being used, manipulated by forces they couldn't see or understand. And the more they uncovered, the more dangerous it became.

Just as Alex was beginning to feel some semblance of security in their grim hideaway, a sound shattered the fragile peace: the unmistakable rumble of a vehicle pulling up outside. Lena's eyes snapped to the door, her body going rigid. Alex's pulse quickened.

"Someone's here," Lena whispered, her voice low but sharp.

Alex stood, his breath catching in his throat. "How did they find us?"

Lena didn't answer. She grabbed her handgun from her bag, silently cocking it as she gestured for Alex to stay behind the table. Her eyes flicked toward the small security camera feed she had set up in the corner of the room, showing the view from outside.

A dark SUV had pulled up, the kind with tinted windows, the kind that belonged to people who didn't want to be seen. And now, the doors were opening. Alex's stomach turned as he saw three men step out, all dressed in black, each one moving with precision and purpose.

"They're professionals," Lena hissed, her voice tight with tension. "This wasn't random. They know exactly where we are."

Alex's heart raced. "What do we do?"

Lena didn't answer. She was already moving, her mind clearly calculating the next steps. She shoved a burner phone into Alex's hand. "You need to go."

"What?" Alex blinked, confused. "I'm not leaving you here."

"You don't have a choice," Lena snapped. "They're here for you. I can hold them off, but you need to get out the back, now."

Alex felt a surge of panic. "I'm not leaving you behind."

"You don't have time to argue!" Lena's voice was fierce, but there was something else in her eyes—fear. Real fear. "I'll be right behind you. But you need to go now."

Before Alex could protest, Lena was already pushing him toward the back door, her eyes locked on the security feed as the men outside approached the front entrance. She glanced back at him once, her expression softening for just a moment. "Trust me, Alex. I'll meet you."

Alex hesitated, torn between wanting to fight and knowing he had no real choice. He nodded, swallowing the lump in his throat, and slipped out the back door into the narrow alley behind the warehouse.

The alley was dark and cold, the walls of the surrounding buildings pressing in on him as Alex hurried down the narrow path. He could hear the muffled sounds of the men breaking into the warehouse behind him, but he forced himself to keep moving. Lena had told him to run, and he trusted her. But every instinct screamed at him to turn back, to fight.

His feet pounded against the pavement as he turned a corner and slipped into another alley, his breath coming in ragged gasps. He didn't know where he was going. All he knew was that he needed to get as far away from the warehouse as possible.

Suddenly, the sound of footsteps echoed behind him, heavy and fast. Alex's heart leaped into his throat. They were on him.

He ran harder, his legs burning as he sprinted down the alley, his mind racing. He couldn't outrun them forever. He needed a plan, but all he had was the burner phone in his pocket and the clothes on his back.

Up ahead, the alley opened into a wider street, and Alex saw his chance. He ducked behind a row of parked cars, crouching low as the footsteps grew louder, closer. He could hear them now—two men, maybe three, speaking in low voices, their footsteps deliberate and controlled.

He held his breath, his heart pounding in his ears as the men passed by, their shadows stretching across the pavement. They didn't see him. Not yet.

Alex waited, his muscles coiled, ready to run. He couldn't stay here. He needed to keep moving.

But as he shifted his weight, his foot hit something—a piece of broken glass on the pavement, the faint sound barely audible but enough to catch the attention of the nearest man. He stopped, his head snapping in Alex's direction.

Alex's breath caught in his throat as the man turned, his hand going to the gun holstered at his side.

There was no time to think. No time to plan.

Alex bolted, sprinting out from behind the cars and into the street, his feet pounding the pavement as the man shouted behind him. Gunshots rang out, echoing off the walls of the surrounding buildings as Alex zigzagged through the streets, his heart racing. He couldn't stop. He couldn't let them catch him.

As he rounded another corner, he heard a voice in his ear—the burner phone, ringing.

Alex fumbled to answer it, his breath coming in ragged gasps. "Hello?"

"Keep running," came Lena's voice, calm but urgent. "I'm on my way."

Chapter 5

Into the Lion's Den

Alex's legs were burning, his lungs on fire as he tore down the alleyways and deserted streets of the industrial district. Lena's voice still echoed in his ear, urging him to keep running, but his mind was spinning. They had to be close. The sound of footsteps echoed faintly behind him, but he couldn't afford to look back. Not now.

He clutched the burner phone tightly, trying to calm his racing thoughts as he spoke into it. "Lena, where are you?"

"I'm almost there," came Lena's voice, crackling through the static of the line. "I've got a bike. Just keep moving."

A bike. Of course. Lena always had a plan, always had some way to slip through the cracks. But Alex wasn't sure how much longer he could keep running. His muscles ached, his body screamed for him to stop, but the image of the men in black—guns drawn, faces cold—was all the motivation he needed to push himself forward.

The streets had become a maze of warehouses, abandoned loading docks, and forgotten rail tracks. The industrial district was practically a ghost town at this hour, and the only sounds were his own laboured breaths and the distant hum of the city far beyond this forgotten corner.

Alex darted into another alley, his shoes splashing through a shallow puddle as he pressed himself against the rough brick wall. He listened for the footsteps, but for now, all he could hear was his own heartbeat pounding in his ears.

"Lena," he whispered into the phone, trying to steady his voice. "I can't keep this up."

"You're almost clear," she said, her voice unwavering. "Two blocks north. I'll be waiting."

Alex swallowed hard, nodding to himself even though she couldn't see him. He wiped the sweat from his brow, taking a quick, steadying breath before pushing off the wall and breaking into a sprint again. His body felt like it was running on fumes, but the adrenaline—the fear—kept him moving.

As he rounded another corner, he saw the tell-tale glow of streetlights ahead. The industrial district was finally giving way to the edge of the city, and with it, an opportunity to disappear into the chaos of the urban jungle.

But he wasn't alone.

From the shadows of a nearby alley, one of the men stepped out—a cold, hard gaze fixed on Alex. He was dressed in black tactical gear, his hand hovering near the holster on his hip. His eyes met Alex's for a brief moment, and in that instant, Alex knew.

He wasn't getting away easily.

The man moved fast, faster than Alex could react. In a blur of motion, he pulled his gun, the barrel aimed squarely at Alex's chest.

Alex's breath caught, his feet frozen to the pavement.

CRACK.

The gunshot echoed off the walls, loud and final, but the bullet never hit its mark. Instead, it ricocheted off the metal frame of a dumpster beside Alex, sending sparks flying. He stumbled back, his heart thundering in his chest as he scrambled to keep his balance.

The man was already closing in, his expression cold, methodical.

And then, a screech of tires.

Alex's head whipped around just in time to see Lena's motorcycle skid into the alley, her figure hunched low over the handlebars. Without hesitation, she leaned into a sharp turn, her bike roaring as she sped toward him.

"Alex! Get on!" she shouted over the roar of the engine.

There was no time to think. Alex lunged forward, his hands gripping the seat of the bike as he swung one leg over and wrapped his arms tightly around Lena's waist. She gunned the throttle, and they shot forward just as another gunshot rang out behind them.

"Hold on!" Lena shouted, her voice barely audible over the wind whipping past them.

Alex tightened his grip, his heart still racing as they sped through the streets, weaving between abandoned cars and debris. Behind them, he could hear the faint sound of the men giving chase, but Lena was fast—faster than they could hope to catch.

The city was a blur of lights and shadows as they raced through the empty streets, the skyscrapers looming overhead like silent sentinels. Alex could feel his pulse pounding in his ears, his mind still reeling from the close call.

"That was too close," he muttered, his voice hoarse.

Lena didn't respond. Her focus was razor-sharp, her eyes fixed on the road ahead. She knew they weren't out of danger yet.

They rode for what felt like hours, winding through the maze of the city until the streets began to change. The tall buildings gave way to smaller, older structures—the kind that had stood for decades, untouched by the city's rapid modernization. The kind of place where people went to be forgotten.

Finally, Lena slowed the bike, pulling into a narrow alley behind an old, run-down building. The brick walls were covered in faded graffiti, and the air smelled of damp concrete and rusted metal. It was the perfect hiding spot—secluded, out of sight, and off the grid.

"We're here," Lena said as she killed the engine and swung her leg off the bike.

Alex dismounted, his legs shaking from the adrenaline. He glanced around, his chest still heaving as he tried to catch his breath. "Where...where are we?"

Lena pulled off her helmet and ran a hand through her hair. "Safe house. Another one of mine. It's not much, but it's off the radar."

Alex nodded, though he wasn't entirely sure how much longer they could keep running. They had been on the move for hours, and he could feel exhaustion settling deep into his bones. But there was no time for rest. Not yet.

Lena led him to the back door of the building, a rusted metal frame that looked like it hadn't been touched in years. She pulled out a small key from her pocket and slid it into the lock, the door creaking open with a low groan.

Inside, the space was small but functional—bare concrete floors, a few old pieces of furniture, and a table covered in maps, documents, and electronic gear. A single lamp cast a dim glow over the room, giving it the feel of an underground bunker.

Alex collapsed into a chair, running a hand through his hair. "Lena...how long do you think we can keep this up?"

She didn't answer right away. Instead, she walked over to the table, her fingers brushing over the maps and documents scattered across the surface. "As long as we need to."

Alex sighed, his exhaustion catching up to him. "We need to figure out who's behind this, Lena. They're not just chasing us. They're hunting us."

"I know," Lena said, her voice low. "And we're going to find out. But we need more than what we have. That USB drive? It's a start, but it's not enough. Kane has layers—protection, people who will take the fall for him if it comes to that."

Alex frowned, leaning forward. "So what do we do? We can't keep running forever."

Lena looked at him, her expression unreadable. "We need to go after someone who knows how Kane's network really operates. Someone inside."

Alex's stomach churned. "And how are we supposed to do that? Everyone who works for Kane is either too scared to talk or too dead to matter."

Chapter 6

A Dangerous Alliance

For a few long seconds, no one spoke. The tension in the dimly lit back room of the bar was thick, suffocating. Detective Samuel Reed sat across from Alex and Lena, his steely gaze shifting between them, calculating. His fingers drummed lightly on the scarred wooden table, his eyes narrowing with every second of silence that passed.

Alex could feel the weight of the moment pressing down on him. They had walked straight into the lion's den, and now they were asking for a deal with one of Kane's most trusted operatives. Reed was a man who had spent years navigating the dark alleys of corruption, and there was no guarantee he would side with them. In fact, he had every reason to turn them over to Kane right then and there.

Lena didn't flinch, though. She kept her eyes locked on Reed, her expression cold, unreadable. She knew how to handle men like him—men who operated in the gray spaces between the law and the criminal underworld. She had dealt with them before, and she understood their motivations better than anyone.

"You're putting a lot of faith in your ability to walk away from this," Reed finally said, his voice low and measured. "If I wanted to, I could have you both dead before you left this room."

Alex tensed, but Lena didn't miss a beat. "If that's what you were going to do, you would have done it already. But you haven't, which means you're here to listen."

Reed's lip curled into a faint smirk, though his eyes remained cold. "You're either brave or stupid, Thompson. I haven't decided which."

"Try desperate," Lena replied. "Because that's what you are, Reed. Kane's empire is cracking, and you know it. You've been in his pocket for years, but you also know what happens when he starts cleaning house. Loose ends get tied up."

Reed's fingers stopped drumming on the table. He leaned back in his chair, crossing his arms over his chest. "And you think you can take Kane down?"

Lena leaned forward, her voice lowering to a razor's edge. "We don't think, Reed. We know. But we need someone who knows how his network works, someone who can give us access to the parts we can't reach."

Reed raised an eyebrow, clearly amused by Lena's confidence. "You're assuming I'm willing to betray him."

"You've been dirty for years, but you're not stupid," Lena shot back. "You know Kane doesn't leave loose ends. When this all falls apart, who do you think he's going to come after? You're not indispensable to him. You're just another piece on the board, and when he's done with you, you'll be the next to go."

Alex watched the exchange, his heart racing. Lena was playing a dangerous game, and every second felt like they were teetering on the edge of disaster. He had read about men like Reed in the file Lena had given him—men who operated on instinct, men who survived by being one step ahead of everyone else. But Reed wasn't just another corrupt cop; he was deeply embedded in Kane's empire, and if they didn't handle this right, he could bring everything crashing down on them.

Reed's eyes flicked to Alex, assessing him. "And what about you, Mercer? You're not like her. You're not cut out for this world."

Alex's jaw tightened, but before he could respond, Lena answered for him. "Alex doesn't have to be. He's not the one betraying Kane."

There was a beat of silence, and then Reed let out a low chuckle. "You've got balls, Thompson. I'll give you that." He paused, his eyes narrowing as he considered his next words. "Alright. I'll help you. But you better make it worth my while, or I swear I'll bury you both."

Alex felt a wave of relief wash over him, though it was quickly tempered by the knowledge of how dangerous this alliance had just become. They weren't just dealing with Kane's men anymore—they were now tangled up with a corrupt cop who was willing to sell out his boss for the right price.

Lena gave Reed a slow nod, her expression unreadable. "You'll get what you need, but we need information first. How does Kane move his money? How does he keep his network secure?"

Reed's eyes gleamed with amusement. "That's what you want? You think knowing where the money goes is going to be enough to take down a man like Kane?"

"It's a start," Lena replied, her voice cool. "We need leverage."

Reed leaned forward, resting his elbows on the table as he spoke in a low voice. "Kane doesn't just move money through his own accounts. He's got half the city on his payroll—politicians, law enforcement, judges. Everyone you think should be stopping him is either working for him or looking the other way. His real power isn't just in his wealth. It's in his connections."

Lena's expression hardened. "And how do we break those connections?"

Reed shrugged. "You don't. Not directly, anyway. Kane's got layers of protection around him. You take out one piece, he's got three more ready to replace it. That's how he's stayed untouchable for so long."

Alex's heart sank. They had known Kane was powerful, but hearing it laid out like this made the scope of his control even more terrifying. It wasn't just about taking down one man—it was about dismantling an entire network of corruption that reached deep into the heart of the city.

"There's got to be a way to weaken him," Lena pressed. "Something we can use to make him vulnerable."

Reed studied her for a moment, then sighed. "There is one way. But it's risky. Kane's got a secret bank account, offshore. It's where he keeps the funds that even his closest allies don't know about. If you can get access to that account, you can cripple him financially."

"And how do we get access?" Alex asked, leaning forward.

Reed's eyes gleamed. "You need someone on the inside. Someone close to Kane who has access to his personal files. And I know just the person."

Alex felt a knot form in his stomach. "Who?"

Reed leaned back in his chair, a slow smile spreading across his face. "His daughter."

The room went silent.

Alex blinked, trying to process what he had just heard. Kane had a daughter? He had read everything there was to know about Marcus Kane's personal and professional life, but there had never been any mention of a daughter.

Lena's expression remained neutral, though Alex could see the gears turning in her mind. "Why haven't we heard about her?"

"Because Kane keeps her hidden," Reed explained. "She's his only real weakness. He doesn't want the world to know about her, and he doesn't want her anywhere near his business. But she's got access to his private accounts. He trusts her."

"And why would she help us?" Lena asked, her voice cold.

Reed's smile widened. "Because she hates him. She's been estranged from him for years, but she still has the keys to the kingdom. You get to her, and she'll give you what you need to take him down."

Alex's mind raced as he tried to piece it all together. It was almost too perfect. Kane's hidden daughter, the one person who could bring his empire crashing down. But it was also dangerous. If Kane found out they were targeting his family, there would be no turning back.

Lena's eyes flicked to Alex, her gaze steady. "We're going to need to find her."

Reed nodded. "I can give you a location. She's off the grid, but she's still in the city. You'll need to be careful, though. Kane's men are always watching, even if she doesn't know it."

Alex's heart pounded in his chest. This was it. The key to everything. But it was also the most dangerous move they had made so far. Going after Kane's daughter meant crossing a line that could never be uncrossed.

"When do we move?" Alex asked, his voice steady but tense.

Lena didn't hesitate. "Tonight."

The night air was thick with tension as Alex and Lena made their way through the winding streets of the city. The lights of downtown gleamed in the distance, but they were far from the glittering towers of TitanTech's headquarters. Here, in the quieter, more residential parts of the city, everything felt still, almost eerie. It was the calm before the storm.

Lena was focused, her mind working through the details of the plan. She had been silent for most of the drive, her hands gripping the wheel tightly as they navigated the narrow streets. Alex could feel the tension radiating off her, but he didn't press her. They both knew what was at stake.

"Reed said she's living under a different name," Lena finally said, breaking the silence. "He gave us an address, but we'll need to be careful. Kane's men could be watching her."

Alex nodded, his stomach twisting with nerves. "Do you think she'll talk to us?"

Lena shrugged. "She might. Or she might turn us over to Kane."

Alex swallowed hard. "And what do we do if she does?"

Lena glanced at him, her eyes hard. "We can't let that happen."

The weight of her words hung in the air, and Alex felt a chill run down his spine. They were walking into unknown territory, and the risks were higher than ever. If Kane's daughter refused to help them—or worse, alerted her father—it would all be over.

But there was no turning back now.

They arrived at the address Reed had given them—a small, unassuming house nestled in a quiet neighbourhood on the outskirts of the city. The street was dark, the only light coming from a single lamppost at the corner. It was the kind of place where nothing ever happened, where people lived quiet, ordinary lives.

Alex's heart raced as they pulled up to the curb. The house looked peaceful, almost too peaceful. There were no signs of Kane's men, no black SUVs parked nearby. But that didn't mean they weren't there, watching from the shadows.

Lena killed the engine and turned to Alex, her expression serious. "We go in quiet. If she doesn't want to help, we leave. No confrontation. Got it?"

Alex nodded, though his nerves were on edge. He wasn't used to this kind of high-stakes game. Every step they took felt like it could be their last.

Lena opened the door and stepped out, moving silently across the street. Alex followed, his heart pounding in his chest. They approached the house cautiously, staying in the shadows as they made their way to the front door.

Lena reached into her bag, pulling out a small device and placing it against the lock. There was a faint click, and the door swung open silently.

Alex swallowed hard as they stepped inside. The house was dark, but the faint glow of a TV could be seen from the living room. Someone was home.

Lena motioned for Alex to stay behind her as they moved through the hallway. Every nerve in Alex's body was on high alert, his senses sharp as they approached the living room.

And then, they saw her.

A woman, in her mid-thirties, sat on the couch, her back to them. Her hair was long and dark, and she was hunched over, staring at something on the coffee table in front of her. She hadn't heard them come in.

Lena took a step forward, her voice calm but firm. "Emily Kane?"

The woman froze, her body tensing as she turned slowly to face them. Her eyes were wide with fear and shock, her hands trembling slightly as she stared at Lena and Alex.

"What...who are you?" she whispered, her voice shaky.

Lena didn't flinch. "We need to talk."

Emily's eyes flicked to the door, her breathing quickening. "Did my father send you?"

"No," Lena said quickly. "We're not here to hurt you. We need your help."

Emily's eyes narrowed, suspicion creeping into her gaze. "Help? With what?"

Alex stepped forward, his voice soft but urgent. "We need to take your father down."

Emily's face paled, her eyes widening with shock. "You...you don't know what you're asking."

Lena's voice was steady. "We know exactly what we're asking."

For a long moment, no one spoke. Emily stared at them, her expression torn between fear and anger. Finally, she shook her head, her voice trembling.

"You don't understand. My father...he's not someone you can take down."

Alex's heart sank, but Lena didn't back down. "He's more vulnerable than you think. And you're the only one who can help us."

Emily's eyes filled with tears, her voice breaking. "If he finds out I'm talking to you, he'll kill me."

Lena took a step closer, her gaze locked on Emily's. "He won't. We'll protect you."

Emily stared at her, her eyes searching Lena's face for any hint of a lie. For a moment, Alex thought she was going to refuse, that she was going to send them away. But then, something in her expression changed. The fear was still there, but beneath it, Alex saw something else—resolve.

Emily took a deep breath, her voice barely above a whisper. "Alright. I'll help you."

"Not everyone," Lena said, her voice quiet but firm. She turned and picked up a file from the table, handing it to Alex. "There's one person who might be willing to talk."

Alex opened the file, his eyes scanning the pages. His brow furrowed as he read the name at the top.

He looked up at Lena, confusion written across his face. "A detective? Why would a cop know anything about Kane's operations?"

Lena crossed her arms, leaning against the table. "Because Reed isn't just any cop. He's been on Kane's payroll for years, working as his inside man in the police department. He knows how the system works, where the bodies are buried. And if we can get to him, he might be our way in."

Alex felt a knot form in his stomach. "And what makes you think he'll talk?"

Lena's eyes darkened. "Because Reed has a problem. He's dirty, but he's not invincible. There are people higher up than him who don't like loose ends, and if Kane goes down, Reed will go with him. He knows it. His only chance is to cut a deal before it's too late."

Alex sat back in his chair, rubbing his temples. "So we're going to blackmail a corrupt cop into helping us take down one of the most powerful men in the country?"

"Basically," Lena said with a shrug.

Alex let out a bitter laugh, shaking his head. "This is insane."

"Welcome to the game," Lena replied dryly.

The plan was set in motion faster than Alex had expected. Lena worked quickly, using her network of contacts to locate Detective Reed and set up a meeting. It was risky—there was no guarantee that Reed would agree to talk, and even if he did, there was no telling if they could trust him.

But they didn't have a choice. The clock was ticking, and every hour they spent running was another hour closer to being caught.

Two days later, they found themselves in the back room of a dingy bar on the outskirts of the city, waiting for Reed to show up. The bar was the kind of place where people went to disappear, the kind of place where no one asked questions.

Alex sat at a small table, his hands fidgeting with a glass of water as he glanced around the room. The air was thick with the smell of cigarette smoke and stale beer, the dim lighting casting long shadows across the walls.

"You nervous?" Lena asked, sitting across from him with her arms crossed.

"Is it that obvious?" Alex muttered.

Lena smirked. "Don't worry. Reed's more scared of us than we are of him."

Alex wasn't so sure about that. From what he had read in the file, Detective Reed was a dangerous man—ruthless, cunning, and loyal to no one but himself. If they were going to make this work, they had to be careful.

The door to the back room creaked open, and Alex's heart skipped a beat as a tall, broad-shouldered man stepped inside. His face was hard, with deep lines etched into his skin from years of stress and corruption. His eyes were sharp, darting around the room before landing on Alex and Lena.

Detective Samuel Reed.

Reed walked over to the table, pulling out a chair and sitting down without a word. He stared at them for a long moment, his expression unreadable.

"You've got a lot of nerve, asking for a meeting like this," Reed said finally, his voice low and gravelly. "What makes you think I won't turn you over to Kane right now?"

Alex's throat tightened, but Lena didn't flinch. She leaned forward, her gaze locked on Reed's. "Because if you were going to do that, you wouldn't have come alone."

Reed's eyes narrowed, but he didn't deny it.

Lena continued, her voice calm but deadly serious. "We know about you, Reed. We know you're on Kane's payroll, and we know you've been feeding him information for years. But what Kane doesn't know is that you're a liability. And if he finds out you've been working with us, you'll be just as dead as we are."

Reed clenched his jaw, his hands resting on the table. "What do you want?"

"We want Kane," Lena said, her voice cold and unyielding. "And you're going to help us take him down."

Reed stared at her for a long moment, the tension in the room thick enough to cut with a knife.

Finally, he spoke, his voice low and dangerous.

"You better have something good, because if this goes south, we're all dead."

Chapter 7

Threads of Betrayal

The moment Emily Kane said the words "I'll help you," the atmosphere in the room shifted. There was a pause—a heavy silence that filled the small living room, as if the entire weight of what she had agreed to had just settled on everyone's shoulders. Emily sat on the edge of the couch, her posture tense, her hands twisting nervously in her lap. Alex could see the fear in her eyes, the conflict tearing at her as she struggled with the decision she had just made.

Lena stood a few feet away, her face impassive, but Alex knew her well enough by now to sense the relief beneath her stoic exterior. They had just made a deal with the one person who could take down Marcus Kane—his own daughter. But the implications of this alliance were huge. If Kane even suspected that Emily was betraying him, it wouldn't just be them in danger—it would be her life on the line as well.

"We need to move quickly," Lena said, her voice cutting through the silence. "Kane's men might already be watching you. If they sense anything's off—if they think you're even considering talking to us—they'll act."

Emily's eyes widened, panic flashing across her face. "I...I didn't know. I thought I was safe. I've stayed out of his business for years. I haven't seen him in months. Why would they be watching me?"

"Because you're still his daughter," Alex said softly. "No matter how far you've distanced yourself from him, you're the only person he truly trusts. And that makes you dangerous to him."

Emily's breath hitched, and she leaned back against the couch, her hands trembling. "I don't want to be involved in this. I left his world for a reason. I thought I could get away from it."

Lena crossed her arms, her eyes hard. "No one gets away from Marcus Kane. You're only safe because he allows you to be. But if he goes down—and believe me, he will—everyone tied to him will fall too. The only way you survive is by helping us take him out."

Alex watched as the fear in Emily's eyes shifted to something else—something more defiant. He could see her wrestling with the decision, weighing her options. She had been living in the shadow of her father's empire for years, and now, for the first time, she was being given a chance to fight back. But it came at an enormous risk.

"What do you need from me?" Emily asked quietly, her voice barely above a whisper.

Lena didn't hesitate. "We need access to his personal accounts. Offshore, encrypted—anything that gives us a financial trail. Reed told us you still have access to some of his files."

Emily bit her lip, her eyes darting to the floor. "I do. He gave me access a long time ago, before everything went dark between us. I never used it, but I kept the passwords, just in case. I...I don't know if they'll still work."

"They'll work," Lena said, her tone firm. "Kane's not the type to change his personal security protocols unless there's a breach. We can use those to start pulling at the threads of his empire."

Emily nodded slowly, though she still looked terrified. "And once you have what you need? What happens then?"

"We take it to the authorities," Alex said, though even as he said the words, he felt a pang of uncertainty. He glanced at Lena, who met his gaze with a sharp look, as if warning him not to say too much.

"The authorities can't always be trusted," Lena added, her voice colder now. "Kane's got people in high places—people who will try to bury this. We need to gather everything first, then decide who to trust."

Emily's hands twisted in her lap, and she nodded. "I understand. But you have to promise me something."

Lena raised an eyebrow. "What?"

Emily's voice trembled as she spoke. "When this is over, when my father goes down, I disappear. I want out. I don't care about the money, I don't care about his empire—I just want to live a normal life, away from all of this."

Lena studied her for a long moment, then nodded. "If you help us take him down, you'll have that chance. But we can't do this without you."

Emily swallowed hard and nodded, the fear still etched in her face. "Alright. I'll do it."

The next few hours were spent meticulously planning their next move. Emily's house had quickly transformed from a peaceful hideaway into a makeshift war room. Lena had brought in equipment from the safe house—a few laptops, burner phones, and an array of encryption tools to ensure that nothing they did could be traced. The walls, once adorned with minimalistic décor, now bore hastily taped-up maps and diagrams of Marcus Kane's network, with lines connecting names, corporations, and offshore accounts.

Alex worked silently, the weight of their situation growing heavier with every passing moment. The reality of what they were about to attempt was sinking in. They weren't just going after a corrupt CEO—they were going after a man who had built an empire of deception, control, and violence. A man who wouldn't hesitate to kill them if he found out what they were doing.

Emily sat at the dining table, her laptop open in front of her, her fingers shaking as she typed in the long-buried passwords that would give them access to her father's private accounts. Lena stood beside her, guiding her through the process, her voice calm but firm, reassuring Emily when she faltered.

"You're doing great," Lena said, her eyes focused on the screen. "Just keep going. We need full access before we can start moving anything."

Emily nodded, her breath shallow as she continued typing. Alex could see the strain in her eyes, the weight of what she was doing pressing down on her. This was more than just a betrayal—it was a final severing of ties between her and her father, a man who had loomed over her life like a dark shadow for as long as she could remember.

"Is it working?" Alex asked, stepping closer to the table.

Lena glanced at him and nodded. "We're in. But it's going to take time to decrypt everything. Kane's not stupid—his accounts are protected by layers of encryption. We're going to have to work carefully."

"Can you do it?" Emily asked, her voice barely above a whisper. "Can you break through it?"

Lena's eyes flashed with determination. "I've broken through worse. It'll take time, but we'll get what we need."

As the hours passed, the tension in the room grew thicker. Every time there was a sound outside—a car passing by, the wind rattling the windows—Alex's heart would jump into his throat. He couldn't shake the feeling that they were being watched, that Kane's men were closing in on them with every minute that passed.

Emily's anxiety was palpable. She had gone from being a terrified bystander to an active participant in the plot to take down her father, and Alex could see the toll it was taking on her. She fidgeted constantly, her eyes darting to the windows, her hands trembling every time she moved to type another password or access another account.

Finally, Lena spoke, her voice breaking the silence. "We've got enough. I've decrypted the first layer."

Alex stepped closer, his heart pounding as he looked at the screen. There it was—account after account, all linked to Marcus Kane. Offshore holdings, hidden investments, millions of dollars flowing through shadow companies. It was a tangled web of corruption, and they were standing on the edge of unraveling it.

"We've got him," Lena whispered, a slow smile spreading across her face. "We've finally got him."

The sense of victory that washed over them was brief, quickly overshadowed by the grim reality of what came next. Now that they had the information, they were more vulnerable than ever. Marcus Kane wouldn't just sit idly by while his empire was threatened. He would strike back—and he would strike hard.

"We need to move fast," Lena said, her voice tense. "The moment we start pulling these accounts, Kane's going to know something's wrong. We'll only have a small window before he locks everything down."

Emily's face paled, and she glanced between Lena and Alex, fear creeping back into her voice. "What do you mean? What happens if he finds out?"

"He'll come after us," Alex said quietly. "And he won't stop until he's destroyed everything."

Emily's eyes filled with panic, and she stood abruptly, pacing across the room. "I...I don't know if I can do this. What if we're wrong? What if he finds out before we're ready?"

"We'll be ready," Lena said firmly. "We've come too far to turn back now."

"But what about me?" Emily asked, her voice trembling. "You said you'd protect me, but what if you can't? What if he—"

"We won't let that happen," Alex interrupted, his voice steady. He moved closer to Emily, his eyes meeting hers. "We're in this together now. We'll protect you."

Emily stared at him for a long moment, her expression torn between fear and something else—something softer, more vulnerable. Finally, she nodded, though the fear in her eyes hadn't diminished.

"I don't want to die for this," she whispered, her voice barely audible.

"You won't," Lena said, her voice sharp. "But you have to trust us."

Emily didn't respond, but she sat back down, her hands still trembling as she resumed working. Alex watched her, his heart heavy with the weight of what they were asking her to do. She was risking everything—her life, her safety—for a chance to bring down her father. And there was no guarantee they would succeed.

The hours ticked by, each one more tense than the last. Lena continued working tirelessly, decrypting more layers of Kane's accounts, uncovering deeper levels of corruption. Alex kept watch by the windows, his eyes scanning the darkened street for any sign of movement. But there was nothing. Just the stillness of the night, the quiet hum of the city beyond.

Suddenly, a sound broke the silence—the unmistakable buzz of a phone vibrating on the table.

Alex's heart jumped, and he turned to see Emily's phone lighting up with an incoming call.

"It's him," Emily whispered, her face going pale as she stared at the screen. "It's my father."

Lena's eyes widened, and she motioned for Emily not to answer. "Don't pick it up. It could be a trap."

But Emily's hand was already trembling as she reached for the phone. "If I don't answer, he'll know something's wrong."

"Emily—" Alex started, but it was too late.

She answered the call.

"Hello?" Emily's voice was shaky, her eyes wide as she listened.

There was a long pause, and Alex could see the fear growing in her expression with every passing second. Whatever Marcus Kane was saying on the other end of the line, it was enough to terrify her.

"No...I haven't...No, I'm fine," Emily stammered, her voice barely above a whisper. "I...Okay, I understand."

Another long pause, and then Emily's face crumpled. "I'm sorry, Dad."

She hung up, her hands shaking violently as she dropped the phone onto the table. Alex rushed to her side, his heart pounding.

"What did he say?" Lena asked, her voice urgent.

Emily's eyes filled with tears, her voice breaking as she spoke.

"He knows."

Time seemed to slow in the seconds after Emily's words sank in. Alex felt his pulse thudding in his ears, a cold wave of dread washing over him. Lena's face went pale, and her sharp, calculated expression shifted into one of pure focus. They had been compromised. Marcus Kane knew what they were doing, and that meant they had only moments before everything came crashing down.

"Pack up. Now," Lena snapped, her voice low but commanding as she started yanking cables out of the laptops and throwing them into her bag.

Alex moved quickly, helping her gather their gear while Emily sat frozen in shock, her face pale, her breath coming in short, panicked gasps.

"He's coming for us, isn't he?" Emily whispered, her eyes wide with fear.

Lena didn't look up from her work, her hands moving in a blur as she packed up the equipment. "Yes. And we need to be gone before he gets here."

Alex glanced out the window, his heart racing. The quiet, residential street outside looked deceptively peaceful, but he knew better. Kane's men could be on their way right now, closing in on them like wolves on the hunt.

"We need to get her out of here," Alex said, his voice tight with urgency. "They'll come for her first."

Lena nodded, her jaw clenched. "I know. We need to move fast."

Emily's eyes filled with tears, her body shaking as she stood from the couch. "I...I can't. I can't do this."

"You don't have a choice," Lena said sharply, grabbing Emily's arm and pulling her toward the door. "We're getting you out of here, and we're doing it now."

The three of them moved quickly, slipping out the back door of the house and into the narrow alley behind it. Alex could feel his heart pounding in his chest as they moved, the adrenaline coursing through him like fire. They had to disappear—now.

But as they reached the end of the alley, a sound stopped them cold.

The unmistakable rumble of an engine.

Alex's stomach dropped as he saw the black SUV pull into the street at the end of the alley. Its headlights flashed in their direction, and Alex's blood ran cold.

"They're here," he whispered.

Lena's face hardened, and she yanked Emily back, shoving her into a side door leading into an old storage building. "Get inside. Now!"

The door slammed behind them, and Alex could hear the footsteps—heavy, deliberate—approaching the alley. They were coming for them.

"They're going to find us," Emily whispered, her voice trembling.

"No, they won't," Lena hissed, pulling out her gun. "Not if we're smart."

Alex's heart raced as he watched Lena's every move, his mind spinning. They had to survive this. They had to escape.

But as the footsteps grew louder, he knew one thing for sure:

They were out of time.

Chapter 8

The Predator's Hunt

Alex's heart pounded as he leaned against the door of the storage building, listening to the low rumble of the black SUV as it idled at the end of the alley. His mind raced, every instinct telling him to run, but he knew there was no way they'd outrun Kane's men now. Not here. Not this close.

Lena's hand rested on her gun, her knuckles white as she surveyed their surroundings, her mind clearly working through every possible escape route. The small, dingy storage building they'd taken refuge in was nothing more than a metal box with a few rusty shelves and dust-covered crates scattered across the floor. It offered little in terms of protection or hiding places, but for the moment, it was all they had.

Emily stood between them, her face pale and her breathing ragged, trembling with fear. Her eyes darted around the room, wide and panicked, as if searching for a way out that didn't exist.

"We can't stay here," Alex whispered, glancing nervously toward the door. "They'll find us any second."

"I know," Lena muttered, her voice low and calm despite the tension. "But we don't move until I say. If we bolt now, we're dead."

Alex swallowed hard, his pulse thudding in his ears. Every fibre of his being screamed for him to run, to find somewhere safer, but he trusted Lena. She had kept them alive this long, and if she said waiting was their best chance, he would listen.

Outside, the footsteps grew closer.

Alex felt a cold wave of fear wash over him as the sounds of heavy boots echoed off the walls of the alley. Kane's men were methodical, moving slowly, taking their time as they approached the building. They weren't rushing in—they were hunting, and they knew exactly where to look.

"Stay quiet," Lena whispered, her voice barely audible. "Don't move."

Emily's hands were shaking violently now, her breathing coming in quick, shallow gasps. Alex placed a reassuring hand on her shoulder, but even he could feel his own fear rising like a tidal wave. Every second that passed felt like an eternity, every creak and groan of the building made his heart race faster.

The footsteps stopped.

For a moment, there was only silence.

Alex held his breath, his entire body tense, waiting for the sound of the door being kicked in or the blast of gunfire. But neither came. Instead, the footsteps resumed, moving away from the building, retreating back into the alley.

"They're leaving," Alex whispered, relief flooding through him.

But Lena shook her head, her expression grim. "No, they're circling around. They're checking for exits."

Alex's stomach twisted. Kane's men were smart. They weren't going to rush in and make mistakes. They were going to take their time, box them in, and cut off every possible escape route.

"We have to move," Lena said suddenly, her voice sharp. "Now."

Without waiting for a response, she grabbed Emily by the arm and pulled her toward the far end of the storage building, where a small window was barely visible behind a stack of old crates. Alex followed closely, his heart racing as they moved quickly and quietly.

Lena reached the window and shoved one of the crates aside, revealing a small but manageable opening. She glanced back at Alex. "We go out here, one at a time. Fast and quiet."

Emily's face paled. "What if they see us?"

"They won't," Lena said firmly. "They're focused on the doors. We go now, while we still have a chance."

Without waiting for further argument, Lena crouched down and slipped through the window with ease, landing softly on the other side. She turned back and motioned for Emily to follow.

Emily hesitated, her hands trembling, but Alex gave her a gentle push. "Go. I'm right behind you."

Emily swallowed hard and climbed through the window, her movements awkward and panicked, but she managed to slip through without making much noise. Alex followed next, his heart pounding as he dropped down onto the cracked pavement outside.

They were in another alley, this one narrower and darker than the last, with towering brick walls on either side. Lena motioned for them to keep moving, and they fell into step behind her, staying close to the shadows as they moved deeper into the maze of alleys that crisscrossed the industrial district.

Alex's legs ached as they continued moving through the narrow alleyways, their breaths coming in short, ragged gasps. Lena led them with the confidence of someone who knew the city's underbelly intimately, turning corners and weaving through side streets as if she had mapped every inch of this part of the city. But no matter how far they ran, Alex couldn't shake the feeling that they were being followed.

Every time he glanced back, he expected to see Kane's men rounding the corner behind them, guns drawn, ready to end it all. But so far, the alleyways remained empty and quiet, save for the distant hum of the city beyond.

Finally, after what felt like hours, Lena slowed her pace and led them into a small, dimly lit courtyard between two dilapidated buildings. She stopped, her hands resting on her knees as she caught her breath.

"We lost them for now," she muttered, wiping sweat from her brow. "But it won't last. We need to get farther out, away from the city."

Alex leaned against the brick wall, his chest heaving. "How far can we go before they catch up?"

Lena glanced at him, her expression unreadable. "As far as we can before they do."

Emily collapsed onto the ground, her body trembling with exhaustion. "I can't...I can't keep going."

Lena crouched beside her, her voice calm but firm. "Yes, you can. You have to."

Emily shook her head, tears streaming down her face. "I don't know how. I'm not like you. I'm not strong."

"You don't have to be strong," Lena said, her voice softening slightly. "You just have to survive."

Alex watched the exchange, his heart aching for Emily. She had been thrown into this nightmare with no warning, no preparation, and now they were asking her to keep running, to keep fighting for her life. He wanted to tell her it would be okay, that they would get through this—but he wasn't sure he believed it himself.

Lena stood abruptly, her face hardening. "We need to keep moving. There's a safe house a few miles from here. We'll hole up there until we figure out our next move."

Emily wiped at her tears and nodded, though her exhaustion was evident in every movement. Alex offered her a hand, helping her to her feet as they prepared to start moving again.

But before they could take another step, the distant roar of an engine shattered the fragile silence.

Lena's eyes flashed with alarm. "Move! Now!"

Without hesitation, they broke into a run, their feet pounding against the pavement as the sound of the engine grew louder. Alex's heart raced, panic surging through him as he glanced back over his shoulder.

A black SUV rounded the corner behind them, its headlights cutting through the darkness like twin beams of death. Kane's men had found them.

"They're coming!" Alex shouted, his voice hoarse.

Lena pushed Emily ahead of her, her eyes scanning the alleyway for any potential escape route. But the narrow, enclosed space offered little in terms of options. They were boxed in, and the SUV was closing fast.

"There!" Lena shouted, pointing to a small metal gate at the end of the alley.

They sprinted toward it, their lungs burning with every step. Alex reached the gate first, his hands fumbling with the latch as the sound of the SUV's engine grew deafeningly loud behind them.

"Hurry!" Emily screamed, panic lacing her voice.

The gate finally gave way, and they tumbled through, slamming it shut just as the SUV screeched to a halt on the other side. They could hear the men shouting, the heavy thud of boots hitting the pavement as they disembarked and started chasing them on foot.

"They're coming on foot," Alex panted, his heart racing.

Lena didn't respond. She grabbed Emily's hand and pulled her forward, leading them through the twisting maze of backstreets and alleyways. They had no time to rest, no time to think. The only thing keeping them moving was the knowledge that if they stopped, they were dead.

Alex's legs felt like lead, his muscles screaming in protest as they continued to run. The adrenaline was wearing off, replaced by the dull ache of exhaustion. Every breath was a struggle, every step a battle to keep going. But the sound of

Kane's men chasing them was a constant reminder that they couldn't stop. Not yet.

"We're almost there!" Lena shouted, her voice breathless.

Alex wasn't sure where "there" was, but he trusted her. She had kept them alive this long, and he wasn't about to question her now.

As they rounded another corner, the narrow alleyway opened up into a larger street lined with old, decrepit warehouses. Lena slowed her pace, her eyes scanning the area for any sign of danger.

"This way," she said, motioning for them to follow her toward a run-down building at the far end of the street.

The building looked abandoned, its windows boarded up and its exterior covered in graffiti. But Alex knew better than to trust appearances. This was Lena's world—a world of secrets, shadows, and hidden safe houses tucked away in the forgotten corners of the city.

They reached the building, and Lena led them to a side door hidden behind a stack of old pallets. She pulled out a small key from her pocket and quickly unlocked the door, ushering them inside.

The interior was dark and musty, the air thick with the smell of damp wood and dust. It was small—just a single room with a few old pieces of furniture scattered about—but it was secure. And for now, that was all that mattered.

Lena locked the door behind them and let out a heavy sigh, her shoulders sagging with exhaustion. "We're safe for now. They won't find us here."

Emily collapsed onto one of the old chairs, her body trembling with exhaustion and fear. "I can't...I can't do this anymore."

Alex sat beside her, his heart aching for her. "We'll get through this," he said, though the words felt hollow. "We just need to hold on a little longer."

Lena crouched down beside them, her eyes hard. "We're not out of this yet. Kane knows we're close, and he's going to throw everything he has at us to stop us."

"What do we do now?" Emily asked, her voice barely a whisper.

Lena's eyes darkened, her voice steady. "We fight back."

The room fell into a heavy silence as Lena's words hung in the air. Alex could feel the weight of the situation pressing down on him, the enormity of what they were about to attempt. They had been running for so long, barely staying one step ahead of Kane's men, but Lena was right. They couldn't keep running forever. Sooner or later, they would have to stand their ground.

But how? Kane had resources, men, and power. They were outnumbered, outgunned, and running out of options.

Lena stood, her eyes cold and determined. "We've got the financial data. We can use it. Kane's empire runs on his ability to pay off the people who protect him. If we can cut off his money, we cripple him."

"How do we do that?" Alex asked, his voice filled with uncertainty. "He'll notice if we start draining his accounts."

Lena nodded. "We don't drain them. We reroute them—send the money to places he can't touch. It'll take time, but once he realizes what's happening, it'll be too late. His power base will start to crumble."

Emily looked up, her face pale. "But he'll come after us. If we hit his finances, he'll know it's us."

"That's why we need to do this carefully," Lena said. "We hit him fast, hard, and then we disappear. We use the data we've gathered to expose him, and once he's exposed, the people who protect him will turn on him. They won't risk going down with him."

Alex felt a chill run down his spine. It was a dangerous plan—a plan that relied on timing, precision, and a whole lot of luck. But it was the only plan they had.

Lena moved to the table, pulling out the laptop she had been using to decrypt Kane's accounts. "We're running out of time. We need to start now."

Emily stood, her body still trembling with fear, but her voice steady. "I'll help."

Alex looked between them, his heart pounding. They were about to go to war with one of the most dangerous men in the world, and there was no turning back.

"Let's do this," Alex said, his voice filled with resolve.

And with that, they set the plan in motion.

Chapter 9

Striking the Empire

The safe house felt like a fortress made of glass—one wrong move, one crack, and the whole fragile structure would shatter around them. Every sound outside the run-down walls made Alex flinch, every passing car sent a wave of adrenaline coursing through his veins. He could feel it, like a cold weight pressing down on his chest: the tension, the danger, the knowledge that Kane's men were out there somewhere, closing in on them. And yet, they had no choice but to stay hidden and fight from the shadows.

Lena sat at the small, wobbly table in the center of the room, her laptop open in front of her. The soft glow from the screen illuminated her face, which was set in an expression of fierce concentration. Her fingers flew over the keyboard, breaking through layers of encryption, accessing one hidden account after another. She was the architect of this takedown, pulling at the strings of Kane's empire, preparing to unravel it all.

Emily hovered nearby, still shaken from the chase but determined to help. She had given Lena access to her father's most secret files, and now, they were about to use those files to dismantle the web of corruption Marcus Kane had spent decades building.

Alex stood near the window, peeking out through the cracked blinds at the darkened street beyond. His heart pounded in his chest, and his body ached from the relentless running. Every instinct screamed at him to keep moving, to get as far away from this nightmare as possible, but he knew that wasn't an option. They were too deep now, and the only way out was through.

"How much longer?" Alex asked, his voice tight with tension as he glanced over at Lena.

Lena didn't look up from the screen. "We're almost there. Just a few more layers to get through."

Alex nodded, but his anxiety didn't ease. They were playing with fire, and the flames were closing in fast.

"I can't believe we're doing this," Emily whispered, her voice barely audible. She paced back and forth, her hands wringing together as she glanced nervously between Lena and Alex. "If my father finds out...I mean, when he finds out..."

"He'll come after us," Alex said, finishing her thought.

Emily's eyes filled with panic, and she stopped pacing, turning to face Alex. "And then what? We keep running forever?"

"We won't have to," Lena interrupted, her voice calm and steady despite the chaos around them. She tapped a few keys and turned the laptop so they could see the screen. "Look."

Alex stepped closer, his heart racing as he saw the numbers displayed on the screen. Millions—no, billions of dollars, spread across dozens of offshore accounts, all linked to Marcus Kane. It was more money than Alex had ever seen in his life, more than he could have ever imagined one man controlling.

"This is it," Lena said, her voice filled with quiet satisfaction. "These are the accounts that keep Kane's empire running. The bribes, the blackmail, the payoffs—everything. We cut off the flow of money, and his entire operation collapses."

Emily stared at the screen, her face pale. "But how do we do that without him finding out?"

Lena's eyes gleamed with determination. "We reroute the funds. Slowly, over the next few hours, I'll transfer the money to accounts he can't access. By the time he realizes what's happening, it'll be too late."

Alex's heart pounded. "And then what?"

"Then we disappear," Lena said simply. "For good."

It sounded so simple. So final. But Alex knew better. Kane wouldn't just let them walk away. He would come after them with everything he had, and even if they succeeded in crippling his finances, they'd still be running for their lives.

"What if he finds us before we finish?" Emily asked, her voice trembling. "What if he already knows?"

Lena's expression hardened. "Then we fight."

Alex's stomach churned. This was it—the point of no return. Once they started draining Kane's accounts, there was no going back. Kane would know. His men would know. And they would come for them, relentlessly and without mercy.

But they didn't have a choice.

"Start it," Alex said, his voice steady despite the fear gnawing at his insides. "Let's finish this."

Lena gave a single nod and turned back to the laptop. Her fingers moved quickly, entering commands, transferring funds from one account to another. The process was slow, methodical, designed to avoid detection for as long as possible. But it wouldn't last. Sooner or later, someone on Kane's team would notice the missing money, and when they did, all hell would break loose.

The minutes dragged on, each one feeling like an eternity. Outside, the night was deathly quiet, the only sound the distant hum of the city far beyond the abandoned streets where they hid. Alex's nerves were frayed, every muscle in his body tense as he waited for the inevitable. He had never been a fighter—he was a data analyst, someone who solved problems with numbers and logic, not violence. But now, as he stood in the shadows of this crumbling safe house, he realized that survival would require more than just intelligence. It would require strength, resilience, and the willingness to do whatever it took to stay alive.

Emily sat across from Lena, her hands still trembling slightly as she watched the numbers on the screen. She had been strong—stronger than Alex had expected—but he could see the cracks starting to form. She was terrified, and who could blame her? They were going up against her father, one of the most powerful men in the country, and if they failed, they wouldn't just lose the fight. They would lose everything.

"We're almost halfway through," Lena said, breaking the silence. Her voice was calm, but there was an edge of tension to it now. She knew as well as Alex did that their time was running out. "Just a little longer."

Alex nodded, though his anxiety only deepened. He moved back to the window, peeking through the blinds once again. The street was still empty, but that didn't mean they were safe. Kane's men could be anywhere, closing in on them with every passing second.

Suddenly, a flash of movement caught his eye.

Alex's heart skipped a beat, and he ducked down, his breath catching in his throat. "Lena, we've got company."

Lena's head snapped up, her eyes narrowing. "How many?"

"I don't know," Alex whispered, his voice tight. "But they're here."

Lena cursed under her breath and stood quickly, moving to the window. She glanced out, her face hardening as she took in the sight of the black SUVs pulling up at the end of the street.

"They're here," Lena confirmed, her voice cold and focused. "Get ready."

Emily's face paled, and she stood from the table, her eyes wide with fear. "What do we do?"

"We hold them off," Lena said, moving quickly to grab her gun. "Alex, help me barricade the door."

Alex moved without thinking, his hands shaking as he shoved an old, heavy cabinet in front of the door. They were outnumbered, outgunned, and there was no way they could fight Kane's men head-on. But they didn't need to win the fight—they just needed to buy time.

"How much longer do you need?" Alex asked, his voice strained as he pushed the cabinet into place.

Lena glanced at the laptop, her face tight with concentration. "Twenty minutes. If we can hold them off for twenty minutes, I can finish the transfers."

"Twenty minutes," Alex repeated, his heart pounding in his chest. "We can do that."

But even as he said the words, he wasn't sure if he believed them.

The first gunshot shattered the stillness of the night like a thunderclap. It echoed off the walls of the safe house, sending a wave of panic through Alex as he ducked behind the table. Bullets rained down on the building, smashing through the boarded-up windows, cracking the walls, and splintering the old wooden furniture.

"Stay down!" Lena shouted, her voice barely audible over the chaos.

Emily screamed, throwing herself to the ground as glass and debris flew through the air. Alex's heart pounded in his ears, and for a moment, all he could hear was the deafening roar of gunfire.

Lena moved quickly, her gun raised as she crouched behind one of the overturned tables. She fired a few shots in return, her face set in a grim expression of determination. "We need to hold them off!"

Alex ducked lower, his body trembling with fear as the gunfire continued. He wasn't built for this—he had never been in a situation like this before, where his life was on the line, where every second could be his last. But Lena had been right: they didn't have a choice.

"Stay down and keep moving!" Lena shouted as another barrage of bullets tore through the walls.

Emily crawled toward Alex, her face streaked with tears, her hands shaking. "We're not going to make it, are we?"

Alex grabbed her hand, squeezing it tightly. "We are. We just have to hold on."

Another gunshot rang out, this one closer. Alex flinched, his heart racing. The walls of the safe house wouldn't hold for much longer. He could hear the boots of Kane's men pounding against the pavement outside, could hear them shouting orders as they closed in.

"We're almost there," Lena called out, her voice strained. "Just keep them back a little longer."

Alex took a deep breath, his mind racing. They needed a plan—something, anything, that would give them the upper hand. He glanced around the room, his eyes landing on the few old gas canisters stacked near the back wall. It was a long shot, but it was all they had.

He crawled over to Lena, his voice urgent. "We need to blow the door. It's the only way to buy more time."

Lena's eyes flicked to the gas canisters, and a slow smile spread across her face. "You're right. Let's do it."

Alex moved quickly, grabbing one of the canisters and positioning it near the door. Lena grabbed another and did the same, her movements quick and precise. Once they were in place, she motioned for Alex and Emily to get back.

"Stay down!" she shouted as she lit the fuse.

There was a brief, tense silence—then the explosion.

The force of the blast shook the entire building, sending debris flying and knocking Kane's men back from the door. Smoke filled the air, and for a brief moment, there was nothing but chaos.

"We've got a few minutes," Lena said, her voice urgent. "Let's finish this."

Alex nodded, his heart racing as he moved back to the laptop. The transfers were almost complete—just a few more accounts, and Kane's empire would begin to crumble.

But time was running out.

Outside, the sounds of the gunfight were intensifying. Kane's men were regrouping, closing in on the building. Alex could hear them shouting orders, could hear the heavy thud of their boots as they advanced.

"We've got to move," Lena said, her voice strained. "We're running out of time."

Emily sat beside Alex, her body trembling with fear. "We're not going to make it."

"Yes, we are," Alex said, his voice filled with resolve. "We just need a little more time."

The minutes dragged on, each one feeling like an eternity. The gunfire outside grew louder, more desperate, and Alex knew they were running out of options. But then, finally, Lena spoke.

"It's done," she said, her voice filled with grim satisfaction. "The transfers are complete."

Alex let out a breath he hadn't realized he was holding. They had done it. They had taken Marcus Kane's empire apart, piece by piece. But the victory was short-lived.

"They're inside!" Emily screamed, her voice filled with terror.

Alex's heart dropped as the door to the safe house burst open, and Kane's men flooded inside, guns raised, faces cold and hard.

"Get down!" Lena shouted, firing her gun as the men stormed the room.

The gunfire was deafening, the walls shaking as bullets flew through the air. Alex grabbed Emily and pulled her down behind one of the overturned tables, his heart racing as he tried to protect her.

Lena fought like a demon, her movements quick and precise as she took down one of Kane's men after another. But there were too many of them, and they were closing in fast.

"We need to get out of here!" Alex shouted over the roar of gunfire.

Lena fired another shot, her face grim. "We're not getting out."

Alex's stomach twisted with fear, but he knew she was right. They were trapped, outnumbered, and outgunned. There was no way they could fight their way out.

But then, just as all hope seemed lost, there was a sudden, deafening crash.

Alex looked up, his heart pounding as he saw the ceiling above them begin to collapse. Kane's men scrambled for cover as debris rained down, and in the chaos, Alex saw their chance.

"Go!" Lena shouted, pushing Alex and Emily toward the back door. "Now!"

Without hesitation, Alex grabbed Emily's hand and ran, his heart racing as they sprinted toward the exit. Behind them, the gunfire continued, but they didn't stop. They couldn't.

They burst out into the night, the cold air hitting them like a shock as they stumbled onto the street. The safe house was collapsing behind them, the sounds of the battle fading into the distance.

They had survived. But the fight wasn't over.

Not by a long shot.

Chapter 10

Into the Abyss

The cold night air hit Alex like a wave as they stumbled out of the collapsing safe house and into the deserted street. His lungs burned, his legs ached, and every breath felt like it could be his last. Behind them, the safe house continued to crumble, the distant sound of gunfire and shouting fading into the distance as Kane's men struggled to recover from the explosion.

For a moment, there was silence. Just the three of them, standing alone in the dark, their bodies trembling with exhaustion and adrenaline.

"We made it," Alex whispered, his voice hoarse as he bent over, trying to catch his breath.

Lena glanced over her shoulder, her eyes narrowed as she scanned the street for any sign of danger. Her face was set in a hard, grim expression, but there was a flicker of relief in her eyes. "For now."

Emily leaned against the side of a building, her body shaking with exhaustion. Her face was pale, and tears streaked down her cheeks. "We're not safe. They'll find us again. They always do."

Alex took a deep breath, forcing himself to stand up straight. His muscles ached, his mind was racing, but they didn't have time to stop. She was right. They were still being hunted.

Lena turned to face them, her voice sharp and steady. "We need to keep moving. Kane's men are regrouping, and we can't stay out in the open."

Alex's stomach twisted at the thought. They had barely survived the last attack, and now they were back on the run, with nowhere to go and no plan in place. But Lena was right—they had to keep moving.

"We need to figure out where to go next," Alex said, his voice filled with tension. "We can't just keep running."

Lena nodded, her eyes narrowing as she thought. "We'll find another safe house. Something farther out. I've got a few contacts who can help us lay low for a while, but we'll need to be careful."

Emily shook her head, her voice trembling with fear. "There's no place we can hide. My father will never stop. He'll find us. He'll—"

"Stop," Lena said, her voice sharp as she grabbed Emily's arm. "We're not dead yet, and we're not giving up. Do you understand?"

Emily stared at her, her eyes wide with fear. For a moment, Alex thought she might break, that the weight of everything they had been through would finally crush her. But then she nodded, her voice barely a whisper. "Okay."

Lena's grip softened slightly, and she gave Emily a reassuring nod. "We'll get through this. But we need to stay focused."

Alex could see the cracks forming in Emily's resolve. She had been strong, braver than anyone could have expected, but the pressure was taking its toll. He felt it too—the constant fear, the exhaustion, the uncertainty of what came next. But they couldn't afford to fall apart. Not now.

"We'll make it," Alex said softly, trying to sound more confident than he felt. "We just need to keep moving."

They moved quickly, sticking to the shadows as they navigated the narrow, deserted streets of the industrial district. The city felt eerie at night—silent, empty, and dangerous. Every corner felt like a trap, every passing car sent a jolt of panic through Alex's chest. He couldn't shake the feeling that Kane's men were closing in, that no matter how far they ran, they would never escape.

Lena led the way, her movements precise and controlled despite the chaos swirling around them. She had taken charge, guiding them through the maze of backstreets and alleys with a confidence that Alex envied. She knew this world, knew how to survive in it. And right now, she was their only hope.

But even Lena couldn't protect them forever. Alex could see the weariness in her eyes, the tension in her shoulders. She was running on adrenaline, pushing herself past her limits. They all were.

They reached the edge of the industrial district, where the crumbling warehouses gave way to the quiet suburbs on the outskirts of the city. It was a stark contrast—an eerie calm settling over the rows of houses, their windows dark, their streets empty. It felt like they had stepped into another world, a world where the chaos of their lives didn't exist.

Lena stopped at the edge of a small park, her eyes scanning the area for any sign of danger. "We'll rest here for a few minutes. Then we'll head to the next safe house."

Alex glanced around, his heart still pounding. The park was small and unremarkable, with a few benches scattered around a patch of grass. It didn't feel safe, but then again, nothing did anymore.

Emily collapsed onto one of the benches, her face pale as she tried to steady her breathing. "I can't...I can't keep going like this."

Lena didn't respond right away. She was watching the street, her mind clearly racing with thoughts of their next move. But Alex could see the strain in her eyes, the way her hands shook slightly as she checked the time on her watch.

"We'll make it," Lena said finally, her voice softer than before. "We just need to stay ahead of them."

Alex sat beside Emily, his heart aching as he watched her struggle to hold it together. She had been through so much—more than anyone should have to endure—and now she was running for her life from the one person who should have protected her. Her own father.

"Emily," Alex said quietly, his voice gentle. "I know this is hard, but we're going to get through it. We just need to stay strong a little longer."

Emily didn't look at him, but she nodded slowly, her hands trembling in her lap. "I never wanted this. I just wanted to be free of him. But now..."

Alex swallowed hard, unsure of what to say. He wanted to promise her that everything would be okay, that they would make it out alive, but he wasn't sure he believed it himself. The weight of what they were up against was crushing, and every step they took seemed to push them deeper into the abyss.

Lena's voice broke through the silence, sharp and urgent. "We need to go. Now."

Alex stood, his heart pounding as he followed Lena's gaze. In the distance, at the far end of the street, a dark figure moved in the shadows. It was faint, almost impossible to see, but Alex knew instantly what it meant.

They had been found.

Without a word, they broke into a run, their footsteps pounding against the pavement as they fled through the quiet streets. Alex's heart raced, his breath coming in ragged gasps as he pushed himself to keep up with Lena. Emily stumbled beside him, her body shaking with exhaustion, but she didn't stop. She couldn't stop.

Behind them, the sound of footsteps grew louder—heavy boots thudding against the pavement, closing in on them with every passing second. Alex's mind raced, panic surging through him as he tried to think of a way out, but there was no time. They had to keep running.

"There's a way out ahead!" Lena shouted, her voice barely audible over the sound of their frantic escape.

Alex looked up, his heart leaping with hope as he saw the narrow alleyway up ahead. If they could make it there, they might be able to lose their pursuers in the maze of backstreets.

But just as they reached the mouth of the alley, a figure stepped out from the shadows.

It was a man—tall, broad-shouldered, with a face that Alex recognized instantly. His heart dropped into his stomach.

It was Detective Samuel Reed.

Lena skidded to a halt, her eyes wide with shock. "What the hell are you doing here?"

Reed's face was cold, his eyes narrowing as he stepped closer. "I told you I'd help you take down Kane. But you've crossed a line."

Alex felt a chill run down his spine. Something was wrong. Reed had been their ally, their inside man, but now there was a dangerous glint in his eyes, a hardness to his expression that sent a wave of fear through Alex's chest.

"You sold us out," Lena said, her voice laced with anger and betrayal.

Reed shrugged, his lips curling into a smirk. "You didn't think I was going to let you take down Kane without a fight, did you? You're a threat to him. But you're also a threat to me."

Alex's heart pounded in his chest as he realized what was happening. Reed hadn't come to help them. He had come to finish them off.

Before Alex could react, Reed reached into his coat and pulled out a gun, levelling it at Lena.

"This ends now," Reed said, his voice cold and final.

Alex's mind raced. Time seemed to slow as he stared down the barrel of the gun, his breath catching in his throat. There was no way out. Reed had them cornered, and Kane's men were closing in from the other direction.

But Lena wasn't going down without a fight.

In a blur of motion, she lunged forward, knocking the gun from Reed's hand and sending it skidding across the pavement. Reed cursed, swinging at her, but Lena was faster. She ducked under his arm, delivering a sharp elbow to his side that sent him stumbling back.

"Run!" Lena shouted, her voice filled with urgency.

Alex grabbed Emily's hand, pulling her toward the alley as Lena fought off Reed. But just as they reached the alleyway, a gunshot rang out.

Alex's heart stopped.

He turned, his breath catching in his throat as he saw Lena stagger back, her hand clutching her side. Blood seeped through her fingers, staining her clothes as she struggled to stay on her feet.

"Lena!" Alex shouted, his voice filled with panic.

Reed stood over her, his gun raised, his face cold and emotionless.

Alex's mind raced. He couldn't leave her. He couldn't just run. But if he stayed, they were all dead.

Emily tugged at his arm, her voice trembling with fear. "We have to go."

Alex hesitated, his heart torn in two. But he knew she was right. If they didn't leave now, they would never make it.

With one last, desperate glance at Lena, Alex turned and ran.

The alley was dark and narrow, the walls closing in around them as they ran. Alex's heart pounded in his chest, his mind racing with fear and guilt. Lena was hurt—maybe dying—and they had left her behind. But there had been no choice. They couldn't fight Reed. They couldn't fight Kane.

They were running for their lives.

Emily stumbled beside him, her breath coming in ragged gasps, but she didn't stop. The fear in her eyes mirrored his own, and Alex knew that they were both thinking the same thing.

They had lost. They had failed.

But they couldn't stop now. Not yet.

The alley opened up into another street, this one lined with darkened shops and closed businesses. Alex slowed, his chest heaving as he tried to catch his breath.

"What do we do?" Emily asked, her voice filled with desperation.

Alex shook his head, his mind blank. "I don't know. I don't—"

Before he could finish, the roar of an engine filled the air.

Alex's heart leapt into his throat as he saw the black SUV turn the corner, its headlights cutting through the darkness. Kane's men had found them.

"Run!" Alex shouted, grabbing Emily's hand and pulling her toward the nearest building.

They sprinted across the street, their footsteps echoing in the night as they ran for cover. The SUV screeched to a halt behind them, and Alex could hear the doors open, could hear the heavy boots of Kane's men hitting the pavement.

They were closing in.

Alex's mind raced, panic surging through him as he searched for a way out. They couldn't keep running forever. They were out of time.

And then, in the distance, he saw it.

A warehouse. Old, abandoned, its windows boarded up, its walls crumbling. It wasn't much, but it was all they had.

"There!" Alex shouted, pointing toward the warehouse.

Emily nodded, her face pale with fear as they sprinted toward the building.

They reached the warehouse just as the first gunshot rang out behind them. Alex threw himself against the door, forcing it open as bullets whizzed past them, shattering the windows and ricocheting off the walls.

"Get inside!" Alex shouted, pushing Emily through the door.

They stumbled into the dark, musty interior of the warehouse, slamming the door behind them just as another volley of gunfire erupted outside.

They were trapped. Cornered. And there was no way out.

Alex's heart raced as he looked around the dimly lit space, his mind spinning with fear and desperation. They couldn't stay here. Kane's men would be on them any second, and there was no way they could fight back.

But they couldn't run, either. Not anymore.

"This is it," Emily whispered, her voice trembling. "This is the end."

Alex shook his head, his hands shaking as he searched for something—anything—that could help them. "No. We're not done yet."

But even as he said the words, he wasn't sure if he believed them.

Because in that moment, as the footsteps outside grew louder, Alex knew one thing for certain:

They were out of time.

Chapter 11

Descent into Darkness

The old, abandoned warehouse was nothing more than a crumbling relic of the city's industrial past, its walls stained with age and neglect. The smell of rust and decay filled the air, and the only light came from the dim shafts of moonlight slipping through cracks in the boarded-up windows. It felt like a tomb—cold, dark, and suffocating. And Alex could feel the weight of it pressing down on him as he and Emily huddled in the shadows, their breaths coming in ragged, terrified gasps.

Outside, the sound of approaching footsteps sent waves of fear crashing through Alex's body. Kane's men were out there, moving in, cutting off every avenue of escape. The warehouse had seemed like a refuge at first—a temporary haven from the relentless chase. But now, it felt like a death trap.

"They're coming," Emily whispered, her voice trembling with fear.

Alex's heart raced as he pressed his back against the wall, his mind spinning. He could hear the distant murmur of voices, the crunch of gravel underfoot as Kane's men closed in on the building. There was no way out. No backup. No hope.

But there was still time. A sliver of time to act.

"We need to find a way to hold them off," Alex said, his voice barely audible over the thudding of his heart.

Emily shook her head, her eyes wide with panic. "There's nowhere to go. We're trapped."

"We're not dead yet," Alex replied, though he wasn't sure if he was saying it to convince her—or himself. His hands were shaking, his breath ragged, but he forced himself to move, scanning the darkened interior of the warehouse for anything—anything—that could give them a fighting chance.

The warehouse was filled with rusted machinery, broken crates, and a scattering of old tools that had been left behind when the building had been abandoned. But it was little more than debris, and Alex knew it wouldn't be enough to hold back Kane's men for long.

Emily crouched behind one of the larger crates, her hands trembling as she hugged her knees to her chest. Her face was pale, her eyes darting toward the windows every few seconds, as if expecting the men to burst through at any moment.

"I never should have helped you," she whispered, her voice cracking. "I never should have gotten involved."

Alex's chest tightened with guilt. He could see the fear in her eyes, the regret. She had risked everything by joining them—betraying her father, putting herself in the line of fire—and now they were both paying the price.

"This isn't your fault," Alex said softly, moving closer to her. "You didn't choose this."

Emily shook her head, tears glistening in her eyes. "Yes, I did. I could have walked away. I could have stayed out of it. But now...now we're going to die because of me."

"We're not going to die," Alex said firmly, though his voice wavered with the uncertainty gnawing at his insides. He knelt beside her, his hand resting on her shoulder. "We're going to get out of this."

"How?" Emily asked, her voice filled with despair. "They've found us. It's over."

Alex opened his mouth to respond, but the sudden sound of a door slamming open froze him in place.

His heart leapt into his throat as the unmistakable sound of boots echoed through the warehouse. The men were inside now, their heavy footsteps reverberating off the concrete floor, their voices low and predatory. Alex could hear them moving through the building, searching—hunting.

"They're close," Emily whispered, her breath hitching.

Alex motioned for her to stay down, his mind racing. They had only seconds before Kane's men found them. He needed a plan—anything to slow them down, to buy more time.

He scanned the room again, his eyes landing on an old workbench near the far wall. It was cluttered with tools, bits of metal, and what looked like an old acetylene torch. His pulse quickened.

"I've got an idea," Alex whispered, motioning for Emily to follow him.

She hesitated, her eyes filled with fear, but she nodded and crept after him, staying low as they moved toward the workbench. Alex's hands shook as he rummaged through the tools, his mind working furiously. He grabbed the torch, checking the fuel level. It was still half full.

"What are you doing?" Emily asked, her voice tense.

"I'm going to rig a distraction," Alex said, his voice tight with concentration. "If I can get this torch to blow, it might slow them down."

Emily's eyes widened. "Blow it? Are you crazy?"

"We don't have a choice," Alex muttered, grabbing a few metal scraps and positioning them near the torch. "It's either this, or we're dead."

Emily bit her lip, her eyes flicking nervously toward the door. "Do you even know what you're doing?"

Alex didn't answer. He didn't need to. He had no idea if it would work, but it was all they had.

The footsteps were getting louder now, closer. Alex could hear the men's voices, low and cold, as they called out to each other, spreading out through the warehouse. They were methodical, searching every corner, every hiding spot.

He set the torch down, adjusting the valve, his heart racing. Sweat dripped down his face as he worked, every second feeling like an eternity.

"Hurry," Emily whispered, her voice trembling.

"I'm almost done," Alex muttered, tightening the final piece.

There was a sudden thud—closer now. One of the men had knocked over something nearby, and Alex knew they were running out of time.

With one last, desperate motion, he jammed a piece of metal into the torch's valve, wedging it open. The gas hissed out in a steady stream, filling the air with its acrid smell.

"Back up," Alex whispered, grabbing Emily's arm and pulling her behind a stack of crates.

They crouched down, their bodies pressed against the cold concrete floor, their breaths shallow and quick. Alex held his breath, waiting, praying that the makeshift bomb would work.

The footsteps grew louder, and then—

BOOM.

The explosion ripped through the warehouse, sending a deafening shockwave through the building. The walls shook, dust and debris raining down from the ceiling as flames shot up from the workbench. The men shouted in alarm, their voices filled with confusion as they scrambled to take cover.

Alex grabbed Emily's hand, pulling her to her feet. "Go! Now!"

They ran, their footsteps echoing off the walls as they sprinted toward the back of the warehouse. The flames from the explosion lit up the room, casting eerie shadows as the fire spread, consuming the old, rusted machinery.

Behind them, Alex could hear the men shouting orders, but the explosion had thrown them off. It wouldn't last long, but it was enough.

They reached the back door of the warehouse, and Alex threw it open, his heart racing. The night air hit them like a cold slap to the face, but there was no time to stop. They had to keep moving.

Outside, the streets were dark and empty, the quiet suburban neighbourhood a stark contrast to the chaos they had just escaped. Alex's legs ached from the running, his lungs burned with exhaustion, but he couldn't stop. Not yet.

"Where do we go?" Emily panted, her voice filled with panic.

Alex looked around, his mind racing. They had no plan, no direction. Lena was hurt—maybe dead—and Kane's men were still hunting them. But they couldn't afford to think about that now. They had to focus on surviving.

"There's a construction site a few blocks away," Alex said, remembering the last time they had passed through the area. "We can hide there."

Emily nodded, though her face was pale with fear. They didn't have any other options.

They ran through the quiet streets, their footsteps pounding against the pavement. Alex's heart raced, his mind spinning with thoughts of Lena. He had left her behind—wounded, bleeding, and alone. The guilt gnawed at him, but he forced himself to push it aside. There was no time for regret. Not now.

As they reached the construction site, Alex felt a flicker of hope. The tall, skeletal frames of half-built buildings loomed in the distance, their shadows stretching across the empty lot like dark sentinels. It was a dangerous place to hide—exposed, unfinished—but it was better than the warehouse.

They slipped through the chain-link fence surrounding the site, the cold metal scraping against Alex's arm as they crawled through a gap. The lot was littered with construction materials—piles of wood, stacks of bricks, and half-built walls that provided little cover but enough to keep them out of sight for the moment.

"This way," Alex whispered, motioning for Emily to follow him.

They moved quickly, darting between the stacks of materials as they made their way deeper into the site. The sound of distant sirens filled the air—police responding to the explosion, or maybe Kane's men closing in—but for now, they were alone.

They reached the base of one of the half-finished buildings, and Alex led Emily inside. The structure was little more than a concrete shell, with exposed beams and unfinished walls, but it was enough to give them a moment of respite.

"We'll hide here for now," Alex said, his voice low. "Just until we figure out our next move."

Emily collapsed onto the ground, her body trembling with exhaustion and fear. "I can't...I can't do this anymore."

Alex knelt beside her, his heart aching. He could see the toll this was taking on her—the fear, the exhaustion, the guilt. She had been strong for so long, but now, it was catching up to her.

"We'll get through this," Alex said softly, though his voice wavered with uncertainty. "We just need to hold on a little longer."

Emily shook her head, tears streaming down her face. "How? How do we keep going? They're going to find us. They're going to kill us."

Alex swallowed hard, his own fear threatening to overwhelm him. He didn't have an answer. He didn't know how they would survive this. But he couldn't let her give up. Not now.

"We'll figure something out," Alex said, though his voice was filled with desperation. "We have to."

The distant sound of approaching sirens grew louder, and Alex's stomach twisted with fear. They had bought themselves a little time with the explosion, but Kane's men were relentless. They wouldn't stop until they had found them.

Suddenly, there was a loud crash outside.

Alex's heart leapt into his throat as he stood, his breath catching in his chest. He moved to the edge of the building, peeking around the corner.

His blood ran cold.

A black SUV had just pulled up at the entrance to the construction site. Kane's men were here.

"We have to go," Alex whispered, turning back to Emily. "Now."

But as they prepared to flee, a new sound cut through the air.

Gunfire. Close. Too close.

Alex froze, his heart racing as the realization hit him. Kane's men weren't the only ones closing in.

Someone else was hunting them.

The gunfire echoed through the construction site, loud and sudden, shattering the fragile silence of the night. Alex's breath caught in his throat, and his heart pounded in his chest as he ducked behind one of the unfinished walls, pulling Emily down beside him.

"What's happening?" Emily whispered, her voice filled with panic.

Alex's mind raced. The gunfire had come from somewhere within the site, but it wasn't aimed at them. Not yet, at least. Someone else had joined the hunt. Someone who wasn't Kane's men.

"I don't know," Alex muttered, his voice tight with fear.

He peeked around the corner of the wall, his eyes scanning the site for any sign of movement. The black SUV was still parked at the entrance, but now, two of Kane's men were lying on the ground, unmoving. A third man crouched behind the vehicle, his gun raised, his eyes darting around in confusion.

Someone was taking them out.

Alex's heart raced as he tried to make sense of it. Who else could be after them? Was it the police? Another faction within Kane's network? Or someone else entirely?

"We need to move," Alex whispered, grabbing Emily's hand. "Now."

They crept through the shadows, staying low as they made their way deeper into the site. The gunfire had stopped, but the tension in the air was thick, electric. Whoever was out there was close—too close.

They reached the far end of the site, where a half-finished stairwell led up to the second floor of one of the buildings. Alex motioned for Emily to follow him, and they climbed the stairs, their footsteps barely audible over the pounding of their hearts.

As they reached the top, Alex froze.

A figure stood at the far end of the floor, silhouetted against the moonlight. Tall, lean, and dressed in dark clothing, the figure moved with a grace and precision that sent a chill down Alex's spine.

It wasn't one of Kane's men. It was someone else. Someone deadly.

The figure turned, and Alex's breath caught in his throat as their eyes met.

The man's face was partially obscured by the shadows, but there was no mistaking the cold, predatory glint in his eyes.

Alex's heart pounded in his chest, and a single thought raced through his mind:

They had just walked into another trap.

Chapter 12

The Silent Assassin

The air on the unfinished second floor of the building was cold, thick with tension. Alex's breath came in shallow gasps as he stared at the figure at the far end of the floor, his heart pounding so loudly he thought it might give them away. The man stood still, his posture unnervingly calm, as if he had been expecting them all along. His face remained partially obscured by the shadows, but the deadly glint in his eyes was unmistakable.

This was no ordinary pursuer. Whoever this man was, he was dangerous—far more dangerous than the men Kane had sent before.

Emily crouched behind Alex, her body trembling with fear. He could feel her shaking, could hear her soft, panicked breaths as they crouched in the shadows, watching the figure who now blocked their only escape route. She had been brave so far, but this was something different. This man wasn't just hunting them. He was hunting them for sport.

"We can't stay here," Emily whispered, her voice barely audible.

"I know," Alex replied, his voice tight with fear. He could feel the weight of the moment pressing down on him, could sense that they were on the edge of something far more dangerous than they had faced before. They had escaped Kane's men, but they had walked straight into the path of a predator.

The man moved suddenly, his steps slow and deliberate as he advanced toward them. There was something unnerving in the way he moved—silent, controlled, like a predator stalking its prey.

Alex's heart raced. They were trapped on the second floor of a half-finished building, with no way out but down. The man would catch them before they even made it to the stairs.

"We need to distract him," Alex whispered, his mind racing as he tried to think of a plan. "If we can get him to move in the opposite direction, we might have a chance to escape."

Emily nodded, though her face was pale with fear. "How?"

Alex scanned the area, his eyes landing on a pile of loose construction debris scattered near the edge of the floor. He motioned toward it. "I'll throw something to the other side of the room. When he goes to investigate, we run for the stairs."

Emily swallowed hard, her eyes wide with terror. "What if he doesn't fall for it?"

Alex didn't have an answer. He didn't know what would happen if the man didn't take the bait. But they didn't have any other options. If they stayed here, they were dead.

He grabbed a small piece of concrete, his hand shaking as he held it in his palm. He had one chance. One throw.

The man continued his slow, deliberate approach, his eyes never leaving the spot where Alex and Emily were hidden. He was close now—too close.

Alex took a deep breath, his heart pounding in his chest, and then threw the concrete as hard as he could toward the far end of the floor.

The piece of concrete clattered across the floor, making a loud noise as it bounced off the exposed beams and hit the far wall with a thud. For a moment, everything was still. Alex held his breath, his heart pounding in his ears.

And then the man turned.

Alex grabbed Emily's arm. "Now!"

They sprinted for the stairs, their footsteps barely audible over the sound of their own frantic breathing. The stairs were narrow and steep, their metal frames creaking under the weight of their hurried escape. Alex could hear the man moving behind them now, his footsteps suddenly faster, more deliberate.

"He's coming!" Emily shouted, her voice filled with panic.

They reached the bottom of the stairs, their hearts racing as they burst out into the open construction site. The night air hit them like a cold slap to the face, but they didn't stop. They couldn't stop.

"We need to hide," Alex said, his voice tight with fear. "He'll catch us if we try to run."

Emily nodded, her face pale as they ducked behind a stack of wooden pallets. Alex could hear the man's footsteps now, echoing through the site as he descended the stairs. He was close—too close.

Alex's mind raced. Whoever this man was, he wasn't one of Kane's ordinary operatives. He was something else entirely. A professional. An assassin.

"We need to lose him," Alex whispered, his voice shaking. "He won't stop until he finds us."

Emily looked at him, her eyes wide with terror. "How do we do that? He's faster than us."

"We make him think we're somewhere else," Alex replied, his mind working furiously. "If we can throw him off our trail, we might have a chance."

They crept through the shadows, staying low as they moved deeper into the construction site. The unfinished buildings loomed around them like dark, skeletal sentinels, their empty windows staring down like hollow eyes. Every creak of the metal beams, every rustle of debris underfoot sent a jolt of fear through Alex's body. The assassin was out there, hunting them, and every second felt like a countdown to their inevitable capture.

As they reached the far end of the site, Alex spotted a large, half-constructed elevator shaft in one of the buildings. It was open, the lift still unfinished, but it led to the underground levels of the building—a place where they could hide, at least temporarily.

"There," Alex whispered, motioning toward the shaft. "We can hide down there."

Emily hesitated, her eyes wide with fear. "What if he follows us?"

"He won't," Alex said, though he wasn't sure if he believed it. "He'll think we ran for the street."

They moved quickly, darting across the open ground and slipping into the elevator shaft. The air inside was cold and damp, the walls rough with exposed concrete. Alex led the way, descending the narrow metal ladder that ran along the side of the shaft. It was dark, but the faint glow of moonlight filtered down from above, casting eerie shadows on the walls.

They reached the bottom of the shaft, their footsteps echoing off the concrete floor as they entered the unfinished basement of the building. The space was large and open, filled with construction equipment and piles of debris. It felt like a maze—dark, disorienting, and full of places to hide.

"We'll wait here," Alex said, his voice low. "He won't find us down here."

Emily nodded, though her face was still pale with fear. She sank to the ground, her back against the cold concrete wall, her body trembling. "I can't do this anymore, Alex. I can't keep running."

Alex crouched beside her, his heart aching. He had pushed her to her limits, forced her into this nightmare, and now she was breaking. He could see it in her eyes—the fear, the exhaustion, the overwhelming sense of hopelessness.

"We'll get through this," Alex said softly, though his voice was filled with uncertainty. "We just need to stay strong a little longer."

Emily shook her head, tears streaming down her face. "He's going to find us. He always finds us."

Alex swallowed hard, his own fear gnawing at him. He didn't have the answers. He didn't know how they would escape this. But he couldn't let her give up. Not now.

"We'll figure something out," Alex said, though his voice wavered. "We have to."

They sat in the darkness, their breaths shallow and quick, their bodies tense with fear. The sound of the assassin's footsteps had faded, but Alex knew he was still out there. Waiting. Watching.

Time seemed to stretch on endlessly, every second feeling like an eternity. Alex's mind raced, trying to think of a plan, but the weight of their situation was crushing. They were trapped, hunted, and out of options.

Suddenly, a faint noise broke the silence—a soft, almost imperceptible creak of metal.

Alex froze, his heart leaping into his throat.

The assassin had found them.

Alex's breath caught in his throat as the creak of metal grew louder, echoing through the dark, empty space. He could hear the faint scrape of boots on concrete, the slow, deliberate footsteps of the assassin as he moved through the basement. He was close—too close.

Emily's eyes widened in terror, and Alex could feel her body trembling beside him. She reached for his hand, her grip tight, her breaths shallow and quick.

"We need to move," Alex whispered, his voice barely audible.

Emily shook her head, her eyes filled with panic. "He'll see us."

"If we stay here, he'll find us for sure," Alex replied, his voice shaking. "We have to move."

They crept through the darkness, their footsteps barely audible over the thudding of their hearts. The basement was like a maze, filled with piles of debris and half-constructed walls. Every step they took felt like it might give them away, but they had no choice. They had to keep moving.

The assassin's footsteps grew louder, more deliberate, as he moved closer to their hiding place. Alex could hear the faint sound of metal clinking—perhaps a weapon. His heart pounded in his chest, and a cold wave of fear washed over him.

Suddenly, a loud crash echoed through the basement.

Alex froze, his breath catching in his throat as the sound reverberated through the empty space. It had come from nearby—too close for comfort. The assassin was close, and he wasn't alone.

"We need to go," Alex whispered, his voice tight with fear. "Now."

But before they could move, a voice cut through the darkness—low, cold, and filled with deadly intent.

"I know you're here."

Alex's blood ran cold. The voice was calm, controlled, and terrifying in its certainty.

The assassin had found them.

Chapter 13

The Predator's Game

"I know you're here."

The assassin's voice echoed through the cold, dark basement like a death sentence. His words were low, calm, and terrifying in their certainty. He wasn't guessing. He knew exactly where they were.

Alex's heart pounded in his chest as he crouched behind the half-built wall, his body pressed against the cold concrete. Emily was beside him, trembling with fear, her breath coming in shallow, panicked gasps. He could feel her hand gripping his arm, her fingers cold and tight with desperation. They had been running for hours—running from Kane's men, running from the assassin—and now they were out of places to hide.

The basement felt like a tomb, cold and silent except for the soft, calculated footsteps of the assassin as he moved through the shadows. His movements were slow, deliberate. He wasn't rushing. He was hunting them, playing a game they couldn't win.

Alex's mind raced. They couldn't outrun him. Not in this dark, enclosed space. The basement was a maze of half-built walls and exposed beams, but it offered little in the way of cover. If they stayed here, the assassin would find them. It was only a matter of time.

"We need to move," Alex whispered, his voice tight with fear.

Emily shook her head, her eyes wide with terror. "He'll see us."

"If we stay here, we're dead," Alex replied, his heart pounding. He glanced around, searching for any possible escape route. There had to be a way out—somewhere they could hide, somewhere they could lose him.

But there wasn't. The walls were closing in, and the assassin was getting closer with every step.

The sound of the assassin's boots against the concrete floor grew louder, more deliberate. He was near now, his shadow stretching out across the floor as he approached their hiding spot. Alex could feel the panic rising in his chest, his heart hammering in his ears.

"We have to go," Alex whispered again, grabbing Emily's hand.

Emily hesitated, fear and doubt flashing across her face. She was frozen, paralyzed by the overwhelming terror of the situation. Alex could see the cracks forming in her resolve, the way her body trembled with fear. She had been strong for so long, but now, it was catching up to her.

"We'll die if we stay here," Alex said, his voice soft but urgent. "We can't give up. Not now."

Emily's eyes flicked toward the shadow moving closer, then back to Alex. Finally, with a shaky breath, she nodded. "Okay."

They crept through the shadows, moving as quietly as possible, their bodies pressed low to the ground. Alex's heart pounded in his chest, each step a careful calculation. The assassin's footsteps echoed behind them, slow and methodical. He wasn't rushing. He knew he had them cornered.

The basement was filled with debris—piles of old construction materials, rusted tools, and half-finished walls that seemed to stretch endlessly. The space felt claustrophobic, the walls pressing in on them as they moved deeper into the maze of concrete and steel.

Suddenly, the assassin's voice broke through the silence again.

"You can run," he said, his voice smooth and unsettling, "but you can't hide."

Alex's blood ran cold. The assassin was toying with them, drawing out the fear, relishing the chase. He was in control, and they were his prey.

They reached the far end of the basement, where a set of old metal stairs led up to the next floor. The stairs were rusted and creaked ominously with every step, but they were the only way out.

Alex motioned for Emily to go first. She hesitated, glancing back toward the sound of the assassin's footsteps, but then she nodded and began to climb. The stairs groaned under her weight, the sound echoing through the basement.

"Hurry," Alex whispered, his heart pounding as he followed her up the stairs.

But just as they reached the halfway point, a loud crash echoed through the basement.

The assassin had found them.

Alex's heart leapt into his throat as he heard the assassin's footsteps quicken, the cold, sharp sound of his boots hitting the concrete as he moved faster now, closing in on them. Alex grabbed Emily's hand, pulling her up the last few steps, his mind racing with fear.

"We have to move!" Alex shouted, his voice filled with panic.

They burst through the door at the top of the stairs, emerging into the ground-level floor of the building. It was as unfinished as the basement, with exposed beams and half-constructed walls, but it was open—far too open. They were completely exposed.

"We can't stay here," Alex muttered, glancing around the room. He could hear the assassin's footsteps echoing up the stairs, getting louder and closer. "We need to find a way out."

But there was no way out. The windows were boarded up, the doors locked or blocked by piles of debris. The only way out was the way they had come in—and the assassin was right behind them.

Alex's heart raced as he scanned the room, searching for anything that could help them. His eyes landed on a large pile of construction materials stacked against one of the walls wooden beams, sheets of metal, and old equipment.

"Help me," Alex said, motioning for Emily to follow him.

They ran to the pile, grabbing the beams and sheets of metal and dragging them toward the door. Alex's arms ached as he lifted the heavy materials, his breath coming in ragged gasps, but he didn't stop. They had to barricade the door—buy themselves some time.

The sound of the assassin's footsteps grew louder, his approach slow and deliberate. Alex could hear the creak of the stairs as he climbed, could feel the weight of his presence pressing down on them.

"Hurry," Emily whispered, her voice filled with fear.

They stacked the beams and metal sheets in front of the door, creating a makeshift barricade. It wouldn't hold for long, but it was all they had. Alex stepped back, his breath ragged as he stared at the door, waiting for the inevitable.

For a moment, there was silence.

And then the door shook violently.

Alex's heart leapt into his throat as the door rattled under the force of the assassin's blows. The barricade held, but just barely. The sound of wood splintering and metal groaning filled the air as the assassin pounded on the door, his voice calm and cold on the other side.

"You can't hide forever," the assassin said, his voice unnervingly steady. "You know that, right?"

Alex's chest tightened with fear. He could hear the amusement in the assassin's voice, the cold, calculated confidence. The barricade wouldn't hold much longer.

"We need to find another way out," Alex whispered, grabbing Emily's arm.

They moved quickly, darting across the open room toward one of the unfinished walls. The assassin was close now—too close. Alex could hear the door splintering behind them, could hear the metal groaning as it began to give way.

Suddenly, the door burst open with a deafening crash.

Alex turned just in time to see the assassin step through the wreckage of the door, his eyes cold and focused as he scanned the room. His movements were calm, controlled, as if he had all the time in the world. He wasn't in a hurry. He knew he had them trapped.

Emily let out a soft gasp, her hand tightening on Alex's arm. "We're not going to make it," she whispered, her voice trembling.

Alex's mind raced. They had no weapons, no way to fight back. But they couldn't give up. Not yet.

"Run," Alex whispered, grabbing Emily's hand.

They sprinted toward the far end of the room, their footsteps pounding against the concrete floor. The unfinished walls offered little cover, but they weaved between the beams, ducking and dodging as they tried to put as much distance between themselves and the assassin as possible.

But the assassin was fast. Too fast.

Alex could hear his footsteps closing in, could feel the cold, predatory gaze of the man on his back as they ran. His heart pounded in his chest, his breaths coming in ragged gasps as he pushed himself to move faster, but it wasn't enough.

The assassin was gaining on them.

Suddenly, there was a loud crash behind them. Alex turned just in time to see the assassin knock over a stack of construction materials, sending debris flying across the floor. The man was relentless, his movements precise and efficient as he closed the gap between them.

"We're not going to make it!" Emily shouted, her voice filled with panic.

Alex's mind raced. They couldn't outrun him. They needed a new plan.

He spotted a large piece of metal scaffolding leaning against the far wall. It was old and rusted, barely held together, but it was heavy. If they could knock it down, it might slow the assassin down—give them a chance to escape.

"This way!" Alex shouted, motioning for Emily to follow him.

They ran toward the scaffolding, their hearts pounding in their chests. Alex grabbed one of the rusted beams, his hands shaking as he pulled with all his strength. The metal groaned and creaked, but it didn't budge.

"Help me!" Alex shouted, his voice filled with desperation.

Emily grabbed the beam, her face pale with fear as they pulled together. The metal groaned louder, the rusted bolts creaking under the strain.

Finally, with a deafening crash, the scaffolding gave way.

The metal beams tumbled to the ground, sending a cloud of dust and debris into the air. Alex grabbed Emily's hand, pulling her away from the wreckage as they ran toward the far side of the room.

But the assassin was already recovering. He moved with terrifying speed, dodging the falling beams with ease as he continued his pursuit.

Alex's heart raced. The scaffolding had only bought them a few seconds, and now the assassin was closing in again. They had no more tricks, no more distractions. They were out of options.

Suddenly, Alex spotted a narrow gap in the wall ahead. It was small—barely big enough for them to squeeze through—but it led to the outside. Freedom.

"There!" Alex shouted, pointing toward the gap. "Go!"

Emily hesitated for only a second before she sprinted toward the opening, her breath coming in ragged gasps. Alex followed close behind, his heart pounding as they squeezed through the narrow gap and burst out into the night air.

They were outside now, in the open construction yard. The cold night air hit them like a shock, but they didn't stop. They ran, their feet pounding against the gravel as they sprinted toward the edge of the site.

But just as they reached the fence, a loud, deafening shot rang out.

Alex froze, his breath catching in his throat as the world seemed to slow around him.

Emily stumbled forward, her body jerking violently as the force of the bullet knocked her off her feet.

"No!" Alex shouted, his voice raw with panic.

Emily hit the ground hard, her body limp and motionless. Alex dropped to his knees beside her, his heart pounding in his chest as he reached for her, his hands shaking.

"Emily!" Alex shouted, his voice filled with desperation. "Emily!"

She didn't respond. Her eyes were closed, her face pale.

Alex's heart raced, his mind spinning. He pressed his hands against her chest, feeling the warm, sticky blood seeping through his fingers.

"Emily, no," Alex whispered, his voice breaking.

But before he could do anything else, the cold, deliberate footsteps of the assassin echoed behind him.

Alex turned, his breath catching in his throat as he saw the assassin standing a few feet away, his gun raised, his face expressionless.

"You thought you could run," the assassin said, his voice cold and steady. "But you were wrong."

Alex's blood ran cold as the assassin took a step closer, the barrel of the gun aimed directly at him.

This was it. There was no way out.

The assassin's finger tightened on the trigger, and Alex closed his eyes, bracing himself for the inevitable.

But just as the shot rang out, something unexpected happened.

A blur of movement—fast, precise—rushed past Alex, slamming into the assassin with a force that sent both men crashing to the ground.

Alex's eyes flew open in shock.

Standing over the assassin was someone he hadn't expected to see again.

Lena.

Her face was pale, her body weak, but she was alive—and she had just saved his life.

Chapter 14

The Edge of Survival

For a long, suspended moment, Alex couldn't process what he was seeing.

Lena, bloodied and weak, stood over the fallen assassin like a ghost returned from the dead. Her breaths came in ragged, shallow gasps, her face pale from the effort it had taken to get here, to save them. Yet, despite the blood seeping through the bandage she had hastily wrapped around her side, her eyes remained sharp—steely with determination, cold with a vengeance that sent chills down Alex's spine.

Lena was alive.

Alex's heart hammered in his chest as he stared at her in disbelief. He had thought she was gone, left bleeding on the cold, cracked pavement when Detective Reed turned on them. But now, here she was, barely standing, but standing nonetheless.

"Lena..." Alex whispered, his voice cracking under the weight of emotion.

She glanced at him briefly, her face hard and focused despite the pain etched into every line. "Get Emily. We don't have much time."

The urgency in her voice snapped Alex out of his shock. He turned to Emily, lying on the ground, her body motionless, her skin pale. Panic surged through him as he knelt beside her, his hands trembling as he checked her pulse.

For a moment, there was nothing—just a cold, terrifying emptiness.

But then he felt it. Faint, weak, but there. A pulse. Emily was still alive.

"She's breathing," Alex said, relief flooding through him. "But she's lost a lot of blood."

Lena's jaw clenched as she took a step toward them, wincing as pain shot through her body. "We need to move. Now. Kane's men will be on us any minute."

Alex's mind raced. The adrenaline pumping through his veins made it hard to think clearly, but Lena was right. They couldn't stay here. The assassin was down, but he wouldn't be out for long, and once Kane's men regrouped, they would be swarmed.

He slipped his arms under Emily's limp body, lifting her gently but quickly. She was light, too light, and the warmth of her blood against his hands only made the situation more dire. Every step he took felt like a race against time, every heartbeat a countdown toward their inevitable capture.

Lena, despite her injury, led the way, her steps determined and quick. They moved through the shadows of the construction site, keeping low and out of sight as they made their way toward a section of the fence where part of the barrier had been torn down.

"We have to get to the car," Lena said through gritted teeth. "I stashed it a few blocks from here. We'll be safer once we're out of the open."

Alex nodded, his breaths coming in short gasps as he carried Emily, the weight of her injury pressing down on his chest like a vice. The car. Safety. It sounded so far away. Too far.

But there was no other choice.

They reached the hole in the fence, slipping through the gap into the deserted street beyond. The night was quiet, unnervingly so, with only the distant sounds of the city far away. But Alex couldn't shake the feeling that they were being watched—that Kane's men were lurking in the shadows, waiting to strike.

"Are you sure we're clear?" Alex asked, glancing nervously over his shoulder.

Lena didn't answer right away. Her hand was pressed tightly against her wounded side, her breath shallow as she scanned the street ahead. "Clear enough for now. Let's move."

They moved quickly, staying close to the sides of the buildings as they made their way through the narrow backstreets of the industrial district. The shadows seemed to stretch longer here, the cold night air biting at Alex's skin as he fought to keep his pace steady, despite the burning ache in his arms and the relentless pounding of his heart.

Emily stirred slightly in his arms, her eyes fluttering open for a brief moment before closing again. She was barely conscious, her breathing shallow and uneven, and Alex could feel the panic rising in his chest again. She needed medical attention—soon.

"How far?" Alex asked, his voice strained from both exertion and fear.

Lena pointed toward an intersection up ahead, where a few old cars were parked along the side of the road. "Just there. Keep going."

The car came into view, an old, nondescript sedan that blended perfectly into the forgotten streets of the industrial district. Lena led them to it, fumbling with the keys as she unlocked the doors.

"Get her in the back," Lena ordered, her voice tight with pain.

Alex carefully laid Emily down in the backseat, propping her head up on his jacket. Her skin was cold, her lips pale, and the sight of her like this sent a wave of fear crashing through him.

"We need to get her to a hospital," Alex said, turning to Lena. "She won't make it otherwise."

Lena shook her head, her expression grim. "We can't go to a hospital. Not with Kane's men on our trail. He's got people everywhere, and the moment we walk through the doors of a hospital, we're dead."

Alex's chest tightened. "Then what? We can't just let her bleed out."

Lena's eyes flicked toward Emily, and for the first time since she had arrived, Alex saw a flicker of uncertainty in her expression. She was torn—caught between the need to protect them and the reality of their situation.

"I know someone," Lena said finally, her voice low. "Someone who can help. But it's risky."

"Riskier than letting her die?" Alex asked, his voice thick with frustration and fear.

Lena didn't answer. Instead, she climbed into the driver's seat, starting the engine with a low growl. "Get in. We'll figure it out on the way."

Alex slid into the passenger seat, his heart racing as the car pulled away from the curb. The streets were dark and empty, but every shadow felt like a threat, every corner a potential ambush.

They drove in silence for what felt like an eternity, the tension in the car thick enough to cut with a knife. Alex kept glancing back at Emily, his heart aching with guilt and fear. She had gotten involved in all of this because of him—because he had pushed her into this dangerous game of betrayal and survival. And now she was paying the price.

"Where are we going?" Alex asked finally, breaking the silence.

Lena kept her eyes on the road, her hands tight on the steering wheel. "There's a doctor. A friend of mine. He operates out of an old clinic downtown. It's not exactly legal, but it's safe."

"Can we trust him?" Alex asked, his voice laced with doubt.

Lena's jaw tightened. "We don't have a choice."

Alex's stomach churned. He didn't like the idea of trusting someone outside their immediate circle, especially not with Emily's life on the line. But Lena was right—they didn't have a choice. Time was running out, and if they didn't get her help soon, she wouldn't survive.

They reached the clinic just before dawn. It was a small, unassuming building tucked away in a forgotten corner of the city, the kind of place that looked abandoned at first glance but carried the weight of stories untold. The windows were dark, the walls cracked and worn, but there was a faint glow of light from inside.

Lena parked the car around the back, pulling into a narrow alleyway that offered a sliver of cover from the prying eyes of the city. She winced as she stepped out of the car, her hand still pressed tightly against her wound, but she waved Alex forward.

"Hurry," she said, her voice strained.

Alex didn't waste any time. He gently lifted Emily from the backseat, her body limp in his arms, and followed Lena toward the back door of the clinic. Lena knocked twice, then three times, a specific rhythm that Alex recognized immediately as a code. Someone inside knew they were coming.

The door creaked open, revealing a man in his early forties, his face lined with exhaustion and wear. He was tall, with dishevelled brown hair and glasses that sat slightly crooked on his nose. He looked at Lena first, then at Emily, and his expression tightened.

"She doesn't have much time," the man said, stepping aside to let them in. "Bring her in quickly."

The inside of the clinic was sparse, dimly lit, and smelled faintly of antiseptic. The walls were lined with old medical equipment, some of it outdated and worn, but functional. Alex laid Emily down on a gurney in the center of the room, his heart racing as the man moved quickly to assess her condition.

"What happened?" the man asked, pulling on a pair of latex gloves as he checked Emily's pulse.

"She was shot," Alex said, his voice thick with fear. "She's lost a lot of blood."

The man nodded, his expression grim but focused. He didn't ask any more questions, and Alex was grateful for that. There wasn't time for explanations. Not now.

Lena leaned against the wall, her face pale with pain as she watched the man work. Alex could see the strain in her body, the way her hand trembled slightly as she pressed against her own wound. She was hurting—badly—but she was pushing through it.

"Can you save her?" Alex asked, his voice barely above a whisper.

The man didn't look up from his work, but his voice was steady. "I'll do what I can. But you need to understand—this isn't a hospital. I don't have the equipment here to fix everything. But I'll keep her alive."

Alex's chest tightened, the weight of the situation pressing down on him. "That's all I'm asking."

The man nodded and moved to inject a syringe into Emily's arm, his movements quick and precise. Alex stepped back, his hands shaking as he watched from a distance. There was nothing more he could do—no more choices to make. All he could do now was wait.

Lena finally sank into a chair near the corner of the room, her face tight with pain as she leaned her head back against the wall. Alex moved toward her, his heart aching at the sight of her like this.

"You need help too," Alex said softly, his eyes flicking to the bloodstain on her side.

Lena waved him off, her voice hoarse. "I'll be fine."

"No, you won't," Alex said firmly. "You're bleeding, Lena. You need to let him look at you."

Lena's jaw clenched, and for a moment, Alex thought she might argue. But then her shoulders sagged, and she let out a shaky breath.

"Fine," she muttered, her voice filled with reluctant acceptance. "But Emily comes first."

Alex nodded, his heart heavy with the weight of everything that had happened. They had been running for so long—running from Kane, running from his men, running from the chaos that had swallowed their lives whole. And now, for the first time, they had stopped.

But it wasn't over. Not yet.

As the man worked to save Emily, Alex sat beside Lena, his mind racing with thoughts of what came next. They were alive—for now. But Kane was still out there, and he wouldn't stop until they were all dead.

"We need a plan," Alex said quietly, his voice filled with determination. "We can't keep running like this. We need to take Kane down."

Lena glanced at him, her eyes sharp despite the exhaustion in her face. "I know."

"And we will," Alex continued, his voice steady. "But we need to hit him where it hurts."

Lena's lips curled into a faint smile, though it was filled with pain and fatigue. "That's the idea."

The room fell into a tense silence, the only sound the faint beeping of the machines and the soft hum of the lights overhead. Alex watched as the man worked on Emily, his heart aching with fear and hope. She was strong—stronger than he had ever realized—but even she had her limits.

They all did.

But they couldn't afford to stop now. Not when they were so close to the end.

Alex's mind raced with thoughts of Marcus Kane—of his empire, his power, and the shadow he cast over their lives. They had come so far, risked so much, and now it was time to finish it. Once and for all.

"We're going to end this," Alex said softly, his voice filled with resolve.

Lena's eyes flicked to him, and for the first time in what felt like forever, there was a flicker of hope in her gaze.

"Yes," she said quietly, her voice steady. "We are."

Chapter 15

The Calm Before the Storm

The dim light in the small clinic flickered softly, casting long shadows over the room as Alex watched the doctor work on Emily. Every now and then, the faint beeping of a heart monitor broke the silence, but it did little to ease the suffocating tension that hung in the air. Time seemed to stretch endlessly, the minutes dragging on like hours as Alex sat at Emily's side, his hands trembling in his lap.

She looked so fragile lying there, her skin pale and her breaths shallow, the wound in her side bandaged but still raw. Her face was peaceful, almost as if she were merely asleep, but Alex knew better. She was teetering on the edge, her body fighting to hold on.

"Will she make it?" Alex asked quietly, his voice barely audible over the steady hum of the machines.

The doctor—whose name Alex still didn't know—didn't look up from his work. His focus was entirely on Emily as he adjusted the IV drip, his expression unreadable.

"She's stable for now," the doctor said finally, his voice calm but grave. "But it was close. The bullet nicked an artery, and she lost a lot of blood. If you'd gotten her here any later..."

Alex didn't need him to finish the sentence. He knew exactly how close they had come to losing her. The thought made his chest tighten, a heavy weight settling over him as he looked at her, guilt gnawing at his insides.

This was all his fault. If he hadn't dragged her into this mess, if he had been more careful, more cautious... Emily wouldn't be lying there, clinging to life.

"She's strong," Lena said from the corner of the room, her voice cutting through the silence.

Alex glanced at her, his heart aching at the sight of her. She was sitting on the edge of a metal chair, her face pale and drawn from her own injuries. The doctor had stitched her wound, but she was clearly still in pain. Yet, even now, there was a fierce determination in her eyes—a resilience that seemed unbreakable, no matter how close to the edge she came.

"She'll pull through," Lena added, her voice steady. "Emily's a fighter."

Alex nodded, though doubt gnawed at him. He wished he could believe it, but after everything they'd been through—after all the close calls, the betrayals, and the violence—he wasn't sure how much fight any of them had left.

He rubbed his hands over his face, exhaustion settling into his bones. He hadn't slept in what felt like days, his mind too consumed with fear, regret, and the growing pressure of what lay ahead. They had reached a brief moment of safety, but it wouldn't last. Kane's men would find them eventually, and when they did, the consequences would be deadly.

"We need to think about what comes next," Alex said, his voice hoarse from fatigue.

Lena didn't respond right away. She was watching him carefully, her sharp gaze cutting through the dim light. Alex could see the wheels turning in her mind, the same thoughts that plagued him—what came next, how they would survive, and more importantly, how they could end this nightmare.

"There's no way we can keep running," Alex continued, his voice gaining strength. "We're running out of places to hide. Kane's people are everywhere, and we're not equipped to fight them off."

Lena shifted slightly, wincing as she adjusted her position. "I know. We can't outrun him forever."

"Then we need to go on the offensive," Alex said, the determination in his voice surprising even him. "We need to hit him where it hurts. And I don't just mean financially. We need to take him down. Permanently."

Lena's eyes darkened, and for a moment, Alex wasn't sure how she would respond. She had always been the pragmatic one, the one who knew the risks, the stakes. But as she sat there, silent and bruised, he saw something in her expression—a flicker of agreement, of shared purpose.

"We can't just take him out," Lena said finally, her voice low but deadly serious. "We have to dismantle everything—his entire network. Otherwise, someone else will just step in and take his place."

Alex nodded. "We've already got a start on that. The financial data we've been collecting—it's enough to expose a lot of his operations. But it's not enough to bring him down completely. We need more."

Lena's gaze narrowed. "More?"

Alex took a deep breath, his heart pounding in his chest. "We need to take the fight directly to him. To Kane himself."

Lena's expression hardened, her lips pressing into a thin line. "That's a suicide mission."

"Maybe," Alex admitted. "But it's the only way. Kane controls everything from behind the scenes. We've been playing defense this whole time, reacting to his moves. But if we can get to him—if we can confront him directly—we can end this. Once and for all."

Lena leaned back in her chair, her eyes narrowing as she considered his words. Alex could see the hesitation in her expression, the doubt. She was right to be cautious. Kane was dangerous, more dangerous than anyone they'd ever faced. But Alex also knew that they couldn't keep running forever. Eventually, they would be caught, and if that happened, they wouldn't survive.

"We can't do this alone," Lena said finally, her voice sharp. "We'll need help."

"Who do we trust?" Alex asked, though the question felt hollow. Trust had been a fleeting concept ever since they discovered the depth of Kane's corruption. Every ally, every connection they had made had been tainted by betrayal. Even Detective Reed, the one man they thought they could count on, had turned against them.

"There are still people out there who want to see Kane fall," Lena said, her voice growing firmer. "People who have been hurt by his empire, who've lost everything because of him. They might not trust us completely, but if we can show them what we have—the financial data, the evidence of his corruption—they might be willing to help."

Alex's mind raced, considering the possibilities. There had to be someone—someone powerful enough to challenge Kane's reach, but still untouched by his influence. They needed someone who had the resources, the connections, and the willingness to go up against one of the most powerful men in the city.

"What about Elena Vasquez?" Alex asked, the name slipping from his lips before he could stop himself.

Lena's eyes snapped to his, her expression unreadable. "Elena?"

"She's been investigating Kane for years," Alex said quickly, his heart pounding. "She's tenacious, and she's not afraid to take risks. If we can get her on our side, she could help us expose everything. The corruption, the bribes, the money laundering—everything."

Lena was silent for a long moment, her expression thoughtful. Alex could see the gears turning in her mind, the way she weighed every option, every possible outcome.

"Elena might be our best shot," Lena admitted finally. "She's got connections in the media, and she's built a reputation as a fearless investigator. If we give her the evidence, she could blow this whole thing wide open."

"But she's also a target," Alex said quietly. "Kane knows who she is. He's tried to take her out before."

"We're all targets," Lena replied, her voice hard. "The question is whether she's willing to put herself on the line again."

Alex nodded, though doubt still gnawed at him. Elena Vasquez had been a thorn in Kane's side for years, but that also meant she was in constant danger. Bringing her into their fight would put her at even greater risk, and Alex wasn't sure if he could live with the consequences if something happened to her.

"We need to talk to her," Lena said decisively. "She's our best chance."

Alex hesitated. "And what if she says no?"

Lena's eyes hardened. "Then we find another way. But right now, we need allies, and she's the closest thing we've got to one."

The room fell into silence again, the weight of their decision settling over them like a heavy shroud. Alex's mind raced, running through every possible scenario, every risk. They were walking a tightrope, balancing on the edge of survival, and one wrong move could send them plummeting into the abyss.

But they couldn't afford to wait any longer. The longer they hesitated, the more time Kane had to tighten his grip, to consolidate his power. They had to act, and they had to act soon.

"We'll go to her," Alex said finally, his voice filled with resolve. "But we need to be careful. Kane's men are everywhere, and we can't afford to make any mistakes."

Lena nodded, though her expression remained grim. "Agreed."

Hours passed before the doctor finally stepped away from Emily's side, wiping his hands on a bloodstained cloth. His face was pale, but his expression was one of grim satisfaction.

"She'll be okay," he said, his voice quiet but certain. "She needs rest, and she'll be weak for a while, but she's stable."

Relief flooded through Alex like a tidal wave, and for the first time in what felt like days, he allowed himself to breathe. Emily was safe—at least for now.

"Thank you," Alex said, his voice thick with emotion.

The doctor nodded, though his eyes remained serious. "You need to keep her out of harm's way. She won't survive another hit like that."

"We'll protect her," Lena said firmly, though Alex could hear the strain in her voice.

The doctor nodded again, then turned to clean up his supplies, leaving Alex and Lena alone with Emily. The room was quiet, the faint beeping of the heart monitor the only sound that broke the silence.

Alex sat beside Emily, watching her chest rise and fall with each slow, steady breath. She was safe—for now—but the danger was far from over.

"We'll leave in the morning," Lena said quietly, her voice low but filled with purpose. "We'll find Elena. And then we'll end this."

Alex nodded, though his mind was still spinning with thoughts of what lay ahead. The road before them was long and filled with danger, but for the first time in a long while, they had a plan. A way forward.

It wasn't over yet.

But they were getting closer.

Chapter 16

A Dangerous Gamble

The soft hum of the heart monitor was the only sound in the room as the night pressed on, its silence broken only by the occasional creak of old floorboards beneath the clinic. Alex sat beside Emily's bed, his eyes heavy with exhaustion but his mind far too alert to rest. His gaze drifted to her pale face, her shallow breathing, and the faint, steady rhythm of her heart displayed on the monitor.

She was stable, but Alex couldn't shake the anxiety gnawing at his insides. Emily was the anchor that had kept him grounded throughout this nightmare, and seeing her so fragile, so close to the edge, made him feel like he was losing control. His mind kept returning to the moment she'd been shot, to the blood, to the helplessness he had felt as he watched her slip away.

It's my fault, he thought, the guilt clawing at him with relentless persistence. He had been the one to bring her into this. He had made her a target. And now, they were barely holding on.

Lena stood by the window, her figure framed by the faint glow of moonlight filtering through the blinds. She had barely moved in the last hour, her arms crossed over her chest, her expression distant. Her face was still pale from the blood loss, and though her wound had been stitched, Alex knew she was far from fully healed. Yet, as always, she stood with a kind of unbreakable resolve, her eyes fixed on the street outside as if she were waiting for the storm to come crashing down on them.

"We're running out of time," Lena said quietly, breaking the silence.

Alex glanced up at her, his own thoughts mirroring hers. Time. It felt like the one thing they didn't have. The clock was ticking, and Kane's reach was growing by the hour. He could feel it, like a tightening noose around their necks.

"Do you really think Elena will help us?" Alex asked, his voice thick with uncertainty.

Lena didn't turn away from the window, her gaze still locked on the shadows beyond. "She's our best chance. Kane's tried to silence her before, but she's survived. She hates him as much as we do."

"And if she says no?" Alex pressed. "If she decides that it's too dangerous?"

Lena finally turned to face him, her expression hard but weary. "Then we figure out another way. But we can't afford to keep running. Kane has people everywhere, and he's not going to stop. He wants us dead, Alex. All of us."

Her words hit him like a punch to the gut. The reality of their situation—the constant threat, the relentless chase—it was suffocating. But Lena was right. They couldn't run forever. If they were going to survive, they had to take the fight to Kane. And that meant making dangerous alliances.

Alex rubbed his hands over his face, feeling the weight of exhaustion settling into his bones. "Do you think she'll be safe here?" He glanced at Emily, his chest tightening with worry.

Lena's gaze softened slightly, her eyes flicking to Emily before returning to Alex. "She'll be safe enough for now. The doctor's a good man. He won't turn us over."

"But he can't protect her if Kane's men come here," Alex said, his voice thick with anxiety. "They'll find us eventually."

Lena sighed, stepping closer to the bed. "We'll be back before that happens. We just need to convince Elena to join us. Once we have her on our side, we'll have the leverage we need to expose Kane's empire."

Alex nodded, though the uncertainty gnawed at him. It felt like a fragile plan, one built on too many unknowns, but they didn't have a choice. Kane was too powerful, too entrenched in the city's underworld for them to take down on their own. They needed someone like Elena, someone with influence, someone who could help turn the tide.

But trusting her—trusting anyone at this point—was a dangerous gamble.

"We leave at dawn," Lena said quietly, her voice breaking through his thoughts. "Rest while you can."

Alex stood, his legs heavy with exhaustion, and moved to the small couch in the corner of the room. He lay down, though sleep felt like a distant possibility. His mind was too full of noise—plans, fears, regrets. But above all, it was the thought of facing Kane that kept him awake. The man who had orchestrated all of this, who had ruined countless lives, was out there, watching, waiting for them to make a mistake.

And Alex knew that when the time came to confront him, it would be the fight of their lives.

The hours passed in a blur of restless sleep and tense silence. When the first rays of dawn began to creep through the cracks in the blinds, Alex sat up, his body stiff and aching. He glanced at Emily, still asleep, her breathing steadier now but her face still pale. He hoped—prayed—that she would stay safe while they were gone.

Lena was already up, her movements slow and deliberate as she checked the gun holstered at her side. Her face was set in a hard, determined expression, though the faint lines of pain around her eyes betrayed the toll her injuries were taking on her.

"Ready?" she asked, glancing at Alex as she strapped the gun to her waist.

Alex nodded, though his stomach churned with a mix of dread and determination. "Let's go."

The doctor emerged from the back room, his face drawn and tired from the long night. He glanced at Emily, then at Alex and Lena. "She'll be fine while you're gone," he said, his voice quiet. "But don't take too long. Kane's men will eventually figure out where you are."

"We won't be long," Lena said, her voice firm. "Thank you for everything."

The doctor nodded, though his expression remained grim. "Good luck."

With a final glance at Emily, Alex followed Lena out the back door of the clinic. The early morning air was cold and crisp, a stark contrast to the heavy tension that hung over them as they made their way to the car parked in the alley.

The drive to Elena Vasquez's office was silent, both of them lost in their own thoughts. The streets were quiet at this early hour, but Alex knew that beneath the surface, danger lurked in every shadow. Kane's network was vast, and it wouldn't take long for his men to track them down again. Time was their enemy, and it was running out fast.

As they neared Elena's office building, a nondescript concrete structure tucked away in a quiet part of the city, Alex's heart began to race. This was it. Their one chance to gain an ally powerful enough to turn the tide in their favour. But it also meant putting their lives—and the fate of their entire mission—in someone else's hands.

"Do you think she'll really help us?" Alex asked, his voice filled with a mix of hope and doubt.

Lena didn't answer right away, her eyes fixed on the road ahead. Finally, she spoke, her voice quiet but firm. "We won't know until we try. But she hates Kane as much as we do. If anyone's willing to take the risk, it's her."

Alex nodded, though the knot of anxiety in his stomach only tightened. There was so much at stake—too much. And if Elena decided not to help, if she turned them away or worse, betrayed them to Kane, it would be the end.

They pulled up to the building, parking in a narrow alley a few blocks away to avoid drawing attention. The early morning light cast long shadows across the street, but the city was beginning to stir to life, the distant sound of cars and pedestrians filling the air.

Lena led the way, her steps steady and purposeful despite the pain she was clearly still in. Alex followed close behind, his heart pounding in his chest as they approached the entrance to the building.

The security here was minimal—Elena was careful, but she didn't operate in a fortress. She relied on her network of contacts and her reputation as a hard-hitting investigative journalist to keep her safe. But Alex knew that even the best reputations couldn't protect someone from a man like Kane.

Lena knocked on the door, a quick, sharp rhythm, and after a tense moment, the door opened.

A woman in her early forties stood in the doorway, her dark hair pulled back into a tight bun, her eyes sharp and calculating. She looked them over, her gaze lingering on Lena's bruises and Alex's tense posture before she spoke.

"Lena," Elena Vasquez said, her voice filled with both surprise and suspicion. "I didn't expect to see you again."

Lena's face was unreadable as she stepped forward. "We need your help."

Elena's eyes narrowed, her sharp mind clearly already working through the implications of their sudden visit. She stepped aside, motioning for them to enter. "Come in. Let's talk."

Elena's office was a cluttered space filled with files, newspapers, and half-finished cups of coffee. The walls were lined with bulletin boards covered in photographs, notes, and articles about various figures of power and corruption in the city. Alex could see Kane's name plastered across several of the documents, underlined and circled in red ink.

They sat around a small, battered table in the center of the room, the tension palpable as Elena leaned back in her chair, her eyes fixed on Lena.

"So," Elena said, her voice sharp. "What's this about? I assume it's not just a social call."

Lena didn't waste any time. "We have evidence that can bring down Marcus Kane. But we need your help to do it."

Elena raised an eyebrow, though she didn't look surprised. "Evidence, huh? You're not the first person to come to me with that claim. Kane has his fingers in a lot of pies, but no one's been able to bring him down yet."

"This is different," Alex interjected, his voice filled with urgency. "We have financial records, proof of his network—bribes, blackmail, everything. But we can't do this alone. If we're going to take him down, we need someone with your reach."

Elena studied him for a long moment, her eyes flicking between him and Lena. Alex could see the gears turning in her mind, the careful calculation of risk and reward. She was a journalist, but she was also a survivor. And going after someone like Kane meant putting everything on the line.

Finally, Elena leaned forward, her expression serious. "Let me see what you've got."

Lena reached into her bag, pulling out a small USB drive and sliding it across the table. Elena took it, plugging it into her laptop, her eyes narrowing as the files opened on the screen.

For several long minutes, the room was silent as Elena scrolled through the documents. Alex's heart pounded in his chest, the tension unbearable. He watched her carefully, waiting for a sign—any sign—that she believed them, that she was willing to help.

Finally, Elena leaned back in her chair, her expression unreadable. "This is good," she said quietly. "Really good."

Alex let out a breath he hadn't realized he'd been holding.

"But," Elena continued, her voice hardening, "this isn't enough to bring down a man like Kane. Not on its own. He has too much power, too many people in his pocket. You take this to the authorities, and it disappears. You take it to the media, and he spins it in his favour."

Lena's jaw tightened. "We know that. That's why we need you. You have the contacts, the resources to get this out to the right people. People who won't just brush it under the rug."

Elena was silent for a long moment, her sharp gaze piercing through them. Finally, she nodded, though her expression remained grim.

"I'll help you," she said, her voice steady. "But you need to understand something. Once we start this, there's no going back. Kane will come after you—after all of us—with everything he has. And if we're not careful, we'll all be dead before this even reaches the light of day."

"We know the risks," Alex said firmly, though his heart pounded with the weight of those words.

Elena stood, her face set with determination. "Then let's get to work."

Chapter 17

The Strategy of War

The weight of Elena's words hung in the air like a storm cloud—there was no going back. Alex felt the gravity of that statement deep in his chest, an almost crushing realization that from this point forward, every move they made could be their last. There was no more room for error, no more time to second-guess their decisions. Marcus Kane would be coming for them with everything he had, and if they didn't strike first, they would never survive.

Elena stood by the cluttered bulletin board, her sharp eyes scanning the files scattered across her desk, a slight frown etched into her features as she connected the pieces of Kane's empire in her mind. She was clearly a woman who thrived in chaos, but even now, Alex could see the tension in her shoulders, the subtle signs that she knew the danger they were stepping into.

"You've really pissed him off," Elena muttered, her eyes narrowing as she reviewed the financial documents Alex and Lena had provided. "This isn't just about money. Kane's built an entire web of corruption that extends far beyond the corporate world. You're dealing with a man who sees himself as untouchable."

Alex shifted uncomfortably in his seat, the weight of his decision sinking in deeper. "We're not just taking down a corporation. We're dismantling an entire empire."

Elena's eyes flicked to him, her gaze sharp. "Exactly. And that's why this won't be easy. Kane has politicians, law enforcement, and private security forces all in his pocket. He's built his power over decades. Taking him down won't just be about exposing his corruption—it'll be about survival."

Lena, sitting on the edge of the desk, her posture tense despite the pain in her side, nodded in agreement. "We've already seen what he's capable of. His reach extends farther than we thought."

Elena crossed her arms over her chest, leaning back slightly as she studied the two of them. "You're playing with fire. Once this goes public, once the wheels are in motion, Kane will stop at nothing to silence you. He's going to send more than just hit men next time. He'll burn down anyone who stands in his way."

Alex's stomach twisted at the thought. Emily, lying in a small clinic, clinging to life, flashed in his mind. They had barely escaped the last encounter with their lives. The next time, Kane wouldn't make the same mistakes. He would send his best, and they wouldn't stop until everyone involved was dead.

"We know the risks," Alex said quietly, though the words felt hollow in the face of the monumental task before them. "But if we don't do this, Kane wins. And if he wins, he'll keep doing this to other people. More lives destroyed. More innocent people caught in his web."

Elena's expression softened slightly, though her eyes remained guarded. She could see the fear in Alex's eyes, the weight of responsibility pressing down on him. But she also saw something else—resolve. It was the same determination that had kept her fighting for so many years, even when the odds were stacked against her.

"All right," she said finally, her voice steady. "We'll need to be smart about this. Careful. We can't just throw everything at him at once. If we want to take down Kane, we need to be strategic. We need to cut off his resources, piece by piece, until he has nothing left."

Lena stood, her face set with grim determination. "Where do we start?"

Elena walked over to the bulletin board, where several photographs and documents were pinned up. She pointed to a photograph of a man—a middle-aged, balding man in a suit with a face that screamed bureaucracy.

"This is Gerald Hartman," Elena said, her tone clipped. "He's one of Kane's biggest assets. A lawyer with deep connections in the corporate and political worlds. He's been covering up Kane's tracks for years. If we can expose him, it'll create a ripple effect that will destabilize Kane's entire network."

Alex leaned forward, studying the photograph. "What do we have on him?"

Elena pulled a file from the stack on her desk, flipping it open to reveal a series of documents detailing financial transactions, meetings, and legal manoeuvrings. "Enough to make him sweat, but not enough to take him down completely. That's where you two come in."

Lena raised an eyebrow. "What's the play?"

Elena glanced between them, her expression serious. "Hartman has a safe house in the outskirts of the city. That's where he keeps all his dirty secrets—files, recordings, blackmail material, everything. If we can get into that safe house, we'll have enough leverage to bring him down. And once he's out of the picture, Kane's network will start to unravel."

Alex's heart raced at the prospect. It was dangerous—insanely dangerous—but it was also their best shot at gaining the upper hand. If they could get to Hartman, if they could expose his role in Kane's empire, it would be a devastating blow.

"How well guarded is this place?" Alex asked, already anticipating the answer.

"Very," Elena replied. "Hartman isn't a fool. He knows how valuable his secrets are. But his security isn't on the same level as Kane's. It's manageable."

"Manageable," Lena repeated, her tone dry. "That's comforting."

Elena shrugged. "You knew this wasn't going to be easy."

Alex ran a hand through his hair, the weight of the decision settling over him like a heavy blanket. "How do we get in?"

Elena smiled faintly, though it was a smile tinged with the knowledge of what was at stake. "I'll take care of the logistics. I have a contact who can help you bypass Hartman's security system. But once you're inside, it's up to you to get the evidence."

Lena and Alex exchanged a glance. This was the first major offensive move they would be taking against Kane—an act that would undoubtedly escalate the danger they were in. But it was also their first real chance to go on the attack, to stop reacting and start dismantling the empire that had hunted them for so long.

"We're in," Lena said, her voice firm.

Elena nodded, though there was a flicker of something in her eyes—concern, maybe even doubt. She had seen what happened to people who went up against powerful men like Kane. But she also knew that without people like Alex and Lena willing to take those risks, nothing would ever change.

"You'll need to move fast," Elena said, her voice taking on a more urgent tone. "Once Kane gets wind that you've hit Hartman, he'll tighten security around the rest of his operation. You won't have long before he retaliates."

Alex's heart pounded, the enormity of what they were about to do sinking in. They were walking into the lion's den, fully aware that the odds were stacked against them. But there was no turning back now.

"When do we go?" Lena asked, her voice filled with resolve.

"Tomorrow night," Elena replied. "That gives us time to prepare. I'll get you the Intel you need. Just make sure you're ready."

Lena nodded, though the exhaustion from her injury was beginning to show. She had been pushing herself hard, too hard, but she wouldn't admit it. Not now. There was too much at stake.

Alex glanced at her, his concern for her well-being growing. "We need to be careful," he said quietly, his voice filled with unspoken worry.

Lena shot him a look, her eyes hard but appreciative. "We don't have the luxury of careful, Alex. We have to act."

He sighed, knowing she was right, but the fear still gnawed at him. They were stepping into a deadly game, one that would either bring Kane to his knees or cost them everything.

After the plan had been laid out and Elena had gone over the details one last time, Alex and Lena found themselves back in the car, the tension between them thick as they drove through the city's early morning traffic. The streets were quiet, the world just beginning to wake up, but the storm brewing in their lives was anything but calm.

Lena was silent, her face set in a determined expression, though Alex could see the fatigue pulling at her. She had been through hell these past few days—shot, hunted, nearly killed—and now they were about to dive headfirst into another fight. He couldn't help but admire her strength, but he also worried about how much longer she could keep going.

"You okay?" Alex asked, his voice gentle, though he already knew the answer.

Lena didn't look at him, her gaze fixed on the road ahead. "I'm fine."

Alex wasn't convinced. "You're still hurt. We could take a little more time, maybe—"

"We don't have time," Lena interrupted, her tone sharp but not unkind. "Kane's closing in, and we're running out of places to hide. We have to move now."

He nodded, though the worry still gnawed at him. "I just don't want you getting hurt again."

Lena's lips curled into a faint, tired smile, though it didn't quite reach her eyes. "Getting hurt is part of the job. You know that."

Alex sighed, his heart heavy with the weight of everything they were facing. "I know. I just...I don't want to lose you, too."

Lena glanced at him, her expression softening for a brief moment. There was something unspoken between them, a shared understanding of the danger they were in, of the stakes they were playing for. They had been through so much together, and now, standing on the edge of the final battle, the bond between them felt stronger than ever.

"We'll get through this," Lena said quietly, her voice filled with quiet resolve. "We have to."

Alex nodded, though the doubt still lingered in the back of his mind. The road ahead was long and filled with danger, but for the first time in a long while, they had a plan. A way forward.

The silence between them felt heavy, but it wasn't the awkward kind of silence that had once filled the space between them when they were strangers. This was the silence of two people who understood the weight of the moment, who understood that the path ahead wasn't guaranteed.

They'd reached a point where they could no longer avoid their fates. The choices they made in the next few days would determine everything—whether they lived or died, whether Kane's empire stood or crumbled.

The car rolled through the quiet streets, the early morning light casting long shadows over the city. Alex stared out the window, watching the world wake up around him, knowing that for them, sleep was a distant luxury.

"We'll be ready," Alex said, his voice more certain than he felt.

Lena glanced at him, and for a moment, her expression softened, the steely edge of determination giving way to something more vulnerable, more human. "I know."

They didn't say anything more as the city passed by in a blur of buildings and streets, but the unspoken understanding between them was

enough.

They would face whatever came next together.

Chapter 18

Walking Into the Lion's Den

The morning sun was creeping higher into the sky by the time Alex and Lena returned to the clinic. The cold bite of the early dawn had given way to a slow warmth, but it did little to ease the tension weighing down on them. They had a plan now—a concrete plan to strike back against Kane—but the danger looming ahead was all too real.

Alex glanced at Lena as they walked inside, her face set in a determined, if not weary, expression. She had been pushing herself harder than ever since they'd made the decision to go after Kane. The exhaustion showed in the lines etched across her face, but she refused to slow down. There wasn't time for rest, not now.

Inside the clinic, the doctor sat quietly in the corner of the small office, reviewing some medical files, while Emily was still asleep on the narrow bed, her chest rising and falling steadily. A wave of relief washed over Alex when he saw her breathing—steady, calm. She was still alive. But for how long? They had to act quickly if they wanted to make sure Emily stayed safe.

Lena paused by Emily's bedside, her eyes scanning over the woman who had become an integral part of their lives. She didn't say anything, but Alex could see the subtle tension in her posture, the way her hand tightened into a fist as if she were grappling with her own guilt.

"How is she?" Alex asked, his voice low.

The doctor looked up, his tired eyes reflecting the strain of the past few days. "Stable. But she's still weak. She'll need time to recover fully."

"We don't have time," Lena muttered, her voice clipped with frustration. She didn't mean to sound harsh, but the urgency in her words was undeniable. "We need to move soon."

The doctor nodded, understanding the gravity of their situation. "I'll keep her safe while you're gone. But you have to be careful. Kane's reach is long. He won't stop until he finds you."

Alex's chest tightened at the thought. Kane's men were relentless. They had already come close to losing everything multiple times, and now, with Emily in such a fragile state, the stakes felt even higher.

"We'll be back before he has the chance," Alex said, though his words felt more like a hopeful reassurance than a certainty.

The doctor gave a small nod, but the tension in the room was palpable. Lena stepped away from Emily's bedside, her eyes narrowing as she turned to face Alex. The intensity of her gaze reflected the same thoughts swirling in his mind—they had to act now. Any hesitation could cost them everything.

"We don't have much time," Lena said quietly. "We need to be ready for tonight."

Alex nodded, his mind already spinning with the details of the plan. Tonight, they would break into Gerald Hartman's safe house, retrieve the evidence that could expose his connection to Kane's corruption, and use it to dismantle one of Kane's strongest assets. It was a crucial step in bringing down Kane's empire, but it was also the most dangerous move they had made yet.

Hartman's safe house was heavily guarded, and breaking in wouldn't be easy. If they were caught, they wouldn't just be fighting Hartman's private security—they would have Kane's entire network breathing down their necks. And they might not survive to tell the tale.

But there was no other option. The evidence in Hartman's safe was their only real leverage against Kane. Without it, they were just running blind.

Lena moved toward the door, her body tense with purpose. "Let's get what we need."

Planning in the Shadows

Elena Vasquez's contact had been more helpful than they expected. By the time Alex and Lena had returned to the car to gather the rest of their equipment, they had a detailed map of Hartman's safe house security system, the layout of the building, and the best way to bypass his high-level protections. It was a fortress, but they had an entry point—a small window of opportunity.

The hours leading up to the operation passed in a blur. Alex and Lena worked tirelessly, reviewing the map, going over the plan, and preparing for the worst. There was little conversation, just the quiet focus that came with the knowledge of how dangerous the mission ahead was. They both understood the stakes, and words felt unnecessary in the face of the looming danger.

By the time the sun began to dip below the horizon, casting the city in a dim orange glow, they were ready.

Alex stood by the small table in the corner of the clinic's back room, laying out the equipment they had gathered: a small bag of lock-picking tools, a series of black-out devices to disable the cameras, and a gun—an old, worn revolver that Lena had insisted they take as a precaution.

"I still don't like the idea of using this," Alex muttered, picking up the gun and turning it over in his hands. He had never been comfortable with weapons, despite the violent world they had been pulled into. Guns had become a necessary evil in their lives, but it didn't make them any easier to hold.

"You don't have to like it," Lena said quietly, standing beside him. "You just have to be ready to use it."

Alex glanced at her, his stomach tightening at the cold edge in her voice. He knew she was right. In the world they were living in, hesitation could get them killed. But that didn't make the thought of pulling the trigger any easier.

Lena's expression softened slightly, and she placed a hand on his shoulder. "We'll get through this. We don't have any other choice."

Alex nodded, though the knot of anxiety in his chest didn't loosen. The mission ahead felt like walking into a trap. Hartman was a slippery man, and if they didn't get what they needed from his safe house, Kane would tighten his grip even more.

"Do you ever think about what happens after this?" Alex asked, his voice quieter now, as he set the gun down on the table.

Lena raised an eyebrow, leaning against the wall. "After we take down Kane?"

"Yeah." Alex glanced at her, his mind racing with thoughts of what their lives had become. "If we survive this…what happens next?"

Lena was silent for a long moment, her eyes narrowing as she considered his question. There was a weight to her expression, a kind of weariness that came with the constant fighting and running. She had been fighting this battle for so long that Alex wasn't sure she even knew how to imagine life without it.

"I don't know," Lena admitted finally, her voice low. "But we can't think about that yet. We still have to get through tonight."

Alex nodded, though his mind was already drifting to the possibilities of what life could be if they succeeded. If Kane was brought down, if the corruption was exposed, could they ever go back to normal? Could they find a way to live in peace after everything they had been through?

"Maybe," Alex said, his voice distant. "Maybe after all of this, we can just...be."

Lena glanced at him, her expression softening for a moment. "Maybe."

It wasn't much, but it was enough for now. They couldn't afford to dwell on what might be. They had to focus on the task ahead—the dangerous, deadly task that could cost them everything.

The drive to Hartman's safe house was silent, the tension between them growing as the city lights blurred past the windows of the car. The air was thick with anticipation, and every passing minute felt like the countdown to an inevitable confrontation. Lena drove with steady hands, her gaze fixed on the road ahead, while Alex mentally replayed the layout of the building, the security system, the route they would take.

They arrived just as the sun fully dipped below the horizon, casting the city in deep shadows. Hartman's safe house sat on the outskirts of the city—a large, modern building hidden behind high walls and layers of security. It looked like an impenetrable fortress, and for a moment, Alex wondered if they were in over their heads.

But there was no turning back now.

"We go in, we get the files, and we get out," Lena said, her voice firm as they pulled up a few blocks away from the building, parking in a secluded alley. "Quick and quiet."

Alex nodded, his heart pounding in his chest. "Quick and quiet."

They stepped out of the car, moving through the shadows as they approached the high wall that surrounded Hartman's estate. The night was quiet, too quiet, and the stillness made the hairs on the back of Alex's neck stand on end. He kept a firm grip on the black-out device in his pocket, ready to disable the cameras the moment they got close enough.

Lena scaled the wall with practiced ease, her movements smooth and calculated. Alex followed close behind, his muscles tense as he hoisted himself over the wall and landed quietly on the other side. The garden surrounding the house was meticulously kept, with manicured hedges and pristine walkways leading up to the entrance. It looked peaceful, almost serene.

But Alex knew better.

They moved quickly, keeping low as they approached the house. Lena took the lead, guiding them toward the side entrance, where the security system was weakest. She disabled the alarm with a few quick, precise movements, and they slipped inside the house without a sound.

The interior was as cold and calculated as the exterior—modern, minimalist, and spotless. It didn't feel like a home. It felt like a place where secrets were buried, and Alex could feel the weight of those secrets pressing down on him as they moved through the darkened hallways.

The air inside was heavy with tension, every creak of the floorboards and soft hum of the ventilation system amplifying the silence around them. Alex's heart pounded in his chest as they neared the door to Hartman's office—the room where the safe was hidden.

Lena motioned for Alex to take out the lock-picking tools, and he quickly went to work, his hands trembling slightly as he worked the tumblers. It took longer than he expected, the silence pressing down on him as each second stretched into an eternity.

Finally, with a soft click, the lock gave way, and the door swung open.

Lena slipped inside, her eyes scanning the room for any sign of movement. It was empty, just as they had hoped. But Alex couldn't shake the feeling that they were being watched—that Hartman knew they were here.

They moved toward the large bookshelf that stood against the far wall, knowing that the safe was hidden behind it. Lena pressed the hidden switch, and the bookshelf slid aside, revealing the cold, metal door of the safe.

"This is it," Lena whispered, her voice low but steady. "We're almost there."

Alex's heart raced as Lena worked quickly to crack the safe, the tension in the air growing with every passing second. His mind raced with thoughts of what they would find inside—documents, files, recordings, proof of Kane's empire. This was their chance to bring it all down.

But as the safe clicked open and Lena began to pull out the files, Alex heard something—a sound that sent a chill down his spine.

Footsteps.

Lena froze, her eyes snapping to the door. Alex's heart pounded in his chest as the sound grew louder—slow, deliberate footsteps echoing through the hallway outside.

Someone was coming.

Chapter 19

The Safe House Showdown

The footsteps were unmistakable—heavy, deliberate, and getting closer. Alex's breath caught in his throat as the sound reverberated through the hallway outside the office, each step bringing whoever it was nearer to their location. His heart pounded against his ribs as adrenaline surged through his veins, every muscle in his body tensing for the inevitable confrontation.

Lena froze beside the safe, her hand hovering over the files she had just pulled out. Her sharp eyes locked onto Alex's, and for a moment, there was a silent understanding between them. They didn't need to speak to know that their plan had just become far more dangerous.

"Hide," Lena mouthed, her voice barely a whisper.

Alex nodded, his pulse racing. Quickly and quietly, they moved to the far corner of the room, positioning themselves behind a large wooden cabinet that stood against the wall. The space was tight, and Alex could feel the cold press of the wall against his back as he crouched low, his breathing shallow. They had to remain perfectly still. One wrong move, one noise, and they'd be discovered.

The footsteps stopped just outside the door.

Alex's heart felt like it was about to burst out of his chest as he strained to hear, his mind racing with possible scenarios. Who was it? One of Hartman's guards? Hartman himself? Or had Kane's men already found out about their infiltration?

He glanced at Lena, who remained impossibly calm despite the rising tension. Her face was set in a mask of concentration, her eyes narrowed as she listened for any sign of what was happening on the other side of the door.

For a long, agonizing moment, there was nothing but silence.

Then the door creaked open.

The soft groan of the hinges sent a cold wave of fear through Alex's body. Whoever it was, they were inside now. He could hear the faint shuffle of boots on the hardwood floor as the intruder moved further into the room, their steps slow and cautious. They knew something was wrong.

Alex held his breath, every nerve in his body screaming for him to stay still, to stay hidden. He could feel the weight of the moment pressing down on him, the knowledge that if they were found now, they wouldn't make it out alive.

The footsteps stopped again, this time near the desk. Alex risked a glance around the edge of the cabinet, his heart leaping into his throat at what he saw.

A man stood in the center of the room, his back to Alex, dressed in a dark suit that was too expensive for a mere guard. His stance was casual, almost too casual, as if he was certain that he held all the power in the room. In his hand, a gun gleamed under the dim light from the overhead fixture.

This wasn't a guard. It was Gerald Hartman.

Alex's blood ran cold as the full weight of their situation hit him. Hartman was here, and he wasn't alone. He could hear the faint murmur of voices outside the office, the subtle movement of more men patrolling the house. The safe house was fully guarded, and they were trapped.

Hartman moved toward the safe, his eyes narrowing as he spotted the open door. His jaw clenched, his hand tightening on the gun as he realized what had happened.

"So," Hartman said quietly, his voice cold and sharp. "It seems we have company."

Alex felt his heart seize in his chest. They had been discovered. There was no turning back now.

Hartman moved toward the desk, his gaze sweeping over the room with an eerie calm. "Whoever you are," he said, his voice steady, "you've made a mistake coming here."

Lena shifted slightly beside Alex, her hand brushing against his as she prepared to move. Alex could feel the tension radiating off her, the careful calculation as she assessed their options. They couldn't stay hidden much longer. Sooner or later, Hartman would find them.

Suddenly, Hartman's phone buzzed in his pocket. He pulled it out, glancing at the screen with a frown before answering.

"What is it?" Hartman asked, his voice low and annoyed.

There was a pause as the person on the other end spoke, their voice too muffled for Alex to make out.

Hartman's expression darkened. "What do you mean the perimeter's been breached?"

Alex's heart skipped a beat. Someone else was here. Was it Kane's men? Had they been followed?

Hartman's grip tightened on the gun as he turned toward the door, his voice sharp. "Lock down the house. No one gets out. I'll deal with this myself."

As soon as Hartman stepped out of the room, Lena sprang into action. She moved quickly to the safe, grabbing the files and stuffing them into her bag with practiced efficiency. There was no time to waste. They needed to get out before Hartman's men locked the place down completely.

"We need to move," Lena whispered, her voice tense but controlled.

Alex nodded, his body humming with adrenaline as they slipped out from behind the cabinet. The hallway outside was empty for now, but they could hear the faint sounds of guards moving through the house, their footsteps quick and purposeful. They didn't have long.

They moved quickly, keeping to the shadows as they made their way through the labyrinth of hallways that made up Hartman's safe house. Alex's heart pounded in his chest, every step a calculated risk as they navigated the building. The tension was suffocating, the air thick with the knowledge that one wrong move could end everything.

Lena led the way, her movements smooth and controlled as she guided them toward the exit. But just as they reached the side door, a voice echoed down the hallway.

"There they are!"

Alex's blood turned to ice as he spun around, his eyes locking onto a group of guards rushing toward them, their guns raised.

"Go!" Lena shouted, shoving Alex toward the door.

They burst through the door and into the garden, the cool night air hitting them like a slap in the face. The sound of gunfire erupted behind them, bullets whizzing past as they sprinted toward the wall that surrounded the estate.

Alex's lungs burned with the effort as they ran, his legs screaming in protest, but he didn't stop. He couldn't stop. They had the evidence, but now they had to survive long enough to use it.

Lena reached the wall first, scaling it with the same ease she had shown when they entered. Alex followed close behind, his muscles trembling with the effort as he hoisted himself over the top.

Just as his feet hit the ground on the other side, a bullet ricocheted off the wall beside him, sending a shower of sparks into the air. He ducked instinctively, his heart racing as he followed Lena into the alley.

"Come on!" Lena shouted, her voice urgent as she waved him forward.

They sprinted down the alley, their footsteps echoing in the quiet night as they ran for their lives. The sound of shouting and gunfire faded behind them, but Alex knew they weren't out of danger yet. Hartman's men would be swarming the streets soon, and it was only a matter of time before they caught up.

As they rounded the corner and reached the car, Alex's mind raced with the weight of everything that had just happened. They had the files. They had the proof they needed to take down Hartman—and by extension, Kane—but the cost had been higher than he had imagined. They were being hunted now, and there was no going back.

Lena jumped into the driver's seat, the engine roaring to life as she slammed the car into gear. Alex barely had time to close the door before they sped off into the night, the city lights blurring past them as they made their escape.

The adrenaline still pumped through his veins, his heart pounding in his chest as they raced through the empty streets. He glanced at Lena, her face set in a grim expression, her knuckles white as she gripped the steering wheel.

For a moment, neither of them spoke, the weight of the situation settling over them like a heavy shroud.

"We did it," Alex said finally, his voice hoarse.

Lena didn't take her eyes off the road, but a small, grim smile tugged at the corners of her mouth. "Yeah," she said quietly. "We did."

But the tension in her voice told Alex that this was far from over. They had the evidence, but now they had to survive long enough to use it.

And with Kane's men closing in on them, that would be the hardest part yet.

Chapter 20

No Turning Back

The night air whipped through the car's open windows, carrying the sharp scent of gasoline and asphalt as Lena pushed the engine to its limit. The city sped past them in a blur of lights and shadows, the roar of the car's engine drowning out the frantic beat of Alex's heart. He gripped the seat, his knuckles white as they raced through the empty streets, each twist and turn making him feel like they were one step ahead of death.

Lena's face was a mask of concentration, her eyes glued to the road as she navigated the narrow streets and back alleys that wound through the city's underbelly. Her grip on the steering wheel was tight, her knuckles pale, but her movements were smooth and controlled, the precision of someone who had been in high-pressure situations far too many times.

Behind them, the lights of Hartman's estate had faded into the distance, but Alex knew they weren't safe yet. The danger was far from over. Kane's men would already be mobilizing, and it wouldn't take long for them to catch wind of what had happened at the safe house. The evidence they had taken—the files, the recordings, everything—was the key to taking down Hartman and, by extension, Kane's entire network. But it was also a target painted on their backs, a reason for Kane to come after them with more force than ever before.

"We need to lie low," Lena said, her voice cutting through the roar of the engine. "They'll be looking for us everywhere. We can't go back to the clinic."

Alex nodded, though his mind was still spinning from the events of the last few hours. The adrenaline was still coursing through his veins, making it hard to think straight. The image of Hartman, standing in his office with the gun in his hand, the cold rage in his eyes, was still fresh in his mind.

"We can't risk going back to Elena either," Alex said, his voice hoarse from the tension. "If Kane finds out she's helping us, he'll go after her too."

Lena glanced at him, her expression grim. "She knew the risks. But you're right. We need to get off the grid."

The car screeched around a corner, the tires skidding briefly on the slick pavement before gripping the road again. They were in the industrial district now, the streets darker, quieter. The buildings around them were old, abandoned warehouses and factories that had long since fallen into disrepair. It was the kind of place no one went unless they had a reason to hide—or a reason to disappear.

"Where are we going?" Alex asked, his pulse still racing as they sped through the deserted streets.

"There's a safe house I used to use a few years ago," Lena replied, her voice tight with focus. "It's off the radar. No one knows about it except me."

Alex felt a small flicker of relief at her words, though the tension in his chest didn't ease. They might be able to hide for a while, but they couldn't stay hidden forever. Sooner or later, Kane's men would find them. And when they did, there would be no more running.

"We need to get that evidence to Elena," Alex said, glancing at the bag that held the files they had taken from Hartman's safe. "It's the only way to take Kane down."

Lena didn't respond right away, her focus still on the road. "We will," she said finally. "But not yet. First, we need to make sure we survive the night."

Alex's stomach churned at the thought. They had come so far—risked so much—and now, with the evidence in their hands, the stakes were higher than ever. But even with the proof of Kane's corruption, they were still outnumbered and outgunned. And they both knew that Kane wouldn't hesitate to kill anyone who stood in his way.

The car finally pulled into a narrow alley between two dilapidated buildings, the engine growling softly as Lena slowed to a stop. The alley was dark, the walls covered in graffiti, but there was no sign of anyone nearby. It was the kind of place that had been forgotten by the city—a perfect place to hide.

"This is it," Lena said, cutting the engine.

They stepped out of the car, the silence of the night pressing down on them as they made their way toward a rusted metal door at the back of one of the buildings. Lena fumbled with the lock for a moment before the door creaked open, revealing a narrow staircase that led down into the darkness.

Alex hesitated at the entrance, his heart pounding. Every instinct in his body was screaming that this was a mistake—that they were walking into another trap. But he trusted Lena. He had to. She was the only reason they had survived this long.

Lena motioned for him to follow, and together they descended into the underground safe house.

The safe house was small, cramped, and smelled faintly of mildew. The air was thick and heavy, the kind of stagnant air that hadn't moved in years. A single dim light bulb flickered overhead, casting long shadows over the cracked concrete walls and the sparse furniture that lined the room. It wasn't much, but it was safe—or at least safer than anywhere else in the city.

Lena moved quickly, her eyes scanning the room as she checked the windows and doors for any signs of tampering. Satisfied that they hadn't been followed, she dropped her bag onto the small table in the center of the room and began sorting through the files they had taken from Hartman's safe.

Alex stood by the door, his body still humming with adrenaline, his mind spinning with thoughts of what they had just done. They had the evidence now, but the cost had been high. They had drawn a line in the sand, and Kane would stop at nothing to erase it.

"How long can we stay here?" Alex asked, his voice hoarse.

"A day, maybe two," Lena replied without looking up. "Long enough to figure out our next move. After that, we'll need to move again."

Alex nodded, though the thought of staying in one place for even a few hours made his skin crawl. He could feel the weight of the danger pressing down on him, the knowledge that they were being hunted.

As Lena sorted through the files, Alex moved to the small window that looked out into the alley. The night was still, the streets outside quiet, but he couldn't shake the feeling that they were being watched. Every shadow seemed to move, every sound amplified in the silence.

"We need to go over this," Lena said, her voice cutting through his thoughts.

Alex turned back to her, his heart still racing. Lena was sitting at the table now, the files spread out in front of her. Her expression was serious, her eyes scanning the documents with the sharp focus of someone who had been doing this for years.

"These files are enough to bury Hartman," Lena said, her voice low. "They detail every dirty deal, every bribe, every cover-up he's been involved in. It's enough to get him disbarred, maybe even thrown in prison."

Alex's heart leapt at her words, though the excitement was tempered by the reality of what they were facing. "And Kane?"

Lena's expression darkened. "Hartman's just a piece of the puzzle. This is enough to weaken Kane's network, but it's not enough to bring him down completely. We need more."

Alex's stomach tightened at the thought. They had risked everything to get these files, and now they were being told it wasn't enough.

"We need to hit Kane directly," Lena continued, her voice hard. "Exposing Hartman is a start, but it won't be enough to stop Kane. He'll recover, and he'll come after us even harder."

Alex swallowed hard, the weight of her words sinking in. "What do we do?"

Lena leaned back in her chair, her eyes narrowing as she considered their options. "We need to find the linchpin of Kane's operation. The one thing that holds his entire empire together. If we can take that out, the rest will crumble."

Alex's mind raced. Kane's operation was massive, spread across multiple industries, with layers of protection built in. Finding the weak point would be like finding a needle in a haystack.

Lena stood, pacing the length of the small room as she spoke. "We start with the people closest to him—his inner circle. If we can find someone who's willing to flip, someone who's afraid of going down with him, we might be able to get what we need."

Alex nodded, though the enormity of the task ahead felt overwhelming. They had the evidence to bring down Hartman, but going after Kane directly would be a whole different kind of fight. And it was a fight they might not survive.

"We'll have to move carefully," Lena said, her voice firm. "Kane's not going to take this lying down. He's going to come after us with everything he has."

Alex's stomach churned at the thought. The image of Emily, still recovering in the clinic, flashed in his mind. She was already a target because of him, and if they continued down this path, she would be in even greater danger.

"What about Emily?" Alex asked, his voice thick with worry. "If Kane finds her..."

Lena's expression softened slightly, and for a moment, the hard edge in her eyes faded. "We'll keep her safe. I'll make sure of it."

Alex nodded, though the worry still gnawed at him. He trusted Lena, but he knew that keeping Emily safe would be nearly impossible if Kane turned his full attention to them. And after tonight, there was no doubt that Kane would be coming after them with everything he had.

"We need to rest," Lena said finally, her voice softer now. "We'll figure out our next move in the morning."

Alex nodded, though his mind was still racing. The adrenaline from the night's events was still coursing through his veins, making it hard to think, let alone sleep. But he knew Lena was right. They needed to rest if they were going to have any chance of surviving what came next.

Lena moved toward the small couch in the corner of the room, sitting down with a heavy sigh. Alex sat across from her, his eyes scanning the small, dimly lit room as the weight of their situation pressed down on him.

For a long moment, neither of them spoke, the silence between them filled with the unspoken understanding of what lay ahead. They had the evidence, but the fight was far from over. Kane was still out there, and they both knew that he wouldn't stop until they were dead.

But for now, they had each other. And that was enough.

Chapter 21

Shadows Closing In

The dim light in the small safe house flickered every few minutes, casting eerie shadows along the cracked walls. Alex sat on the edge of the old wooden chair, his eyes trained on the single window in the corner of the room. The safe house felt too small, too confined. Every breath he took seemed to echo in the cramped space, each second dragging like a weight pulling him deeper into the cold pit of fear gnawing at his insides.

They were safe—for now. But Alex knew that the illusion of safety wouldn't last. Kane's reach extended far beyond the city's limits, and after their raid on Hartman's safe house, there was no doubt that Kane was mobilizing his forces, tightening his grip, and preparing to strike back.

Alex leaned his head against the cool concrete wall, his mind spinning with thoughts of what was to come. The files they had stolen from Hartman were valuable—enough to weaken his legal standing, enough to cause cracks in Kane's carefully crafted empire—but Lena had been right. It wasn't enough to bring Kane down completely. They needed more, and the clock was ticking. Every hour they spent hiding was another hour Kane had to close in on them.

Across the room, Lena sat with her back against the wall, her eyes closed but her body tense, like a coiled spring ready to snap at any moment. She hadn't spoken much since they'd arrived at the safe house, but Alex knew that her mind was constantly calculating, always one step ahead. She was the reason they were still alive, and though her face was unreadable, Alex could sense the weight of the burden she carried.

"You should sleep," Lena said, her voice breaking the heavy silence. She didn't open her eyes but spoke with the calm authority that had kept them alive for so long.

Alex glanced at her, surprised. Sleep seemed impossible with the adrenaline still coursing through his veins, his nerves frayed and on edge. "I can't," he admitted quietly. "Not yet."

Lena opened her eyes and gave him a long, measured look. Her expression was soft, almost understanding. "You'll need your strength," she said, her voice quieter now. "We both will."

Alex nodded, but the idea of sleep felt foreign, like something that belonged to a different life—a life before Kane, before the constant danger and fear. He leaned forward, resting his elbows on his knees as he stared at the floor. His mind kept drifting back to Emily, lying in that clinic, unaware of how close the danger was getting. Every time he closed his eyes, he saw her face, pale and weak from the blood loss. She had gotten involved in this because of him. If anything happened to her, Alex wasn't sure he could live with himself.

"I keep thinking about Emily," Alex admitted, his voice thick with guilt.

Lena's eyes softened, and for a moment, the hard edge in her expression faded. "She'll be safe for now," Lena said. "The doctor knows how to keep her hidden."

"But what if Kane finds her?" Alex pressed, the anxiety tightening his chest. "What if he sends his men to the clinic?"

Lena sighed, sitting up straighter. "If Kane wanted her dead, he would have done it already. She's a pawn to him, a way to get to you. As long as she's useful, she's safe."

Alex's stomach churned at the thought. He hated the idea of Emily being used as leverage, as a pawn in Kane's deadly game. But Lena was right. As long as Kane saw value in her, Emily would be spared—for now.

"We'll get her out of this," Lena said firmly, her voice filled with quiet determination. "But we have to take Kane down first."

Alex nodded, though the enormity of the task ahead weighed heavily on him. Kane wasn't just a corrupt businessman—he was a puppet master, controlling politicians, law enforcement, and the criminal underworld with ease. Taking him down would require more than just evidence. They would need to dismantle the entire structure of his empire.

"We need to find his weak point," Alex said, echoing Lena's words from earlier. "Something that will destroy his entire operation."

Lena leaned forward, her eyes sharp and focused. "We'll need to start with his inner circle. Someone close to him, someone with enough dirt to bury him. Hartman was just a cog in the machine. We need someone who's integral to his operation."

Alex thought for a moment, running through the names they had gathered from the files. Hartman, while powerful, wasn't close enough to Kane to bring him down directly. They needed someone higher up, someone with direct access to Kane's most closely guarded secrets.

"There's one name that keeps coming up in the files," Lena said, pulling a sheet of paper from the pile on the table. "Veronica Lyons."

Alex frowned. The name sounded familiar, but he couldn't place it.

"She's a fixer," Lena explained. "Kane's personal problem solver. She handles the messes that people like Hartman can't. Blackmail, disappearances, cover-ups. If anyone has the dirt on Kane, it's her."

Alex's heart skipped a beat. Veronica Lyons. He had heard whispers about her before—rumours of her involvement in high-profile disappearances and political scandals. She was a ghost, operating in the shadows, erasing problems before they became public knowledge. If they could get to her, if they could convince her to turn on Kane, they might have a real chance at taking him down.

"How do we find her?" Alex asked, his pulse quickening with the possibility.

Lena's eyes darkened. "That's the hard part. She's been off the radar for months. Kane keeps her hidden, moving her around the city to avoid detection. But I have a contact—someone who might be able to help us track her down."

Alex nodded, though the idea of chasing down someone as dangerous as Veronica Lyons made his stomach churn. They were stepping into even more dangerous territory, but they didn't have a choice. Kane was tightening his grip, and if they didn't strike soon, they would be swallowed by the very machine they were trying to dismantle.

"When can we meet with your contact?" Alex asked, the tension in his voice betraying his anxiety.

Lena glanced at the old clock hanging crooked on the wall. "Tomorrow morning. He'll meet us at a warehouse near the docks. But we'll have to be careful. Kane's men are probably watching every move we make."

Alex's heart pounded at the thought of what they were about to do. The next step in their plan was critical, but it was also dangerous. If Kane suspected they were going after someone like Veronica Lyons, he would retaliate with full force. And they might not survive the fallout.

Morning Comes with Tension

The night passed in a haze of restless sleep, Alex's mind plagued by nightmares of Kane's men closing in, of Emily slipping away, of Lena disappearing into the shadows. When he finally opened his eyes, the pale light of dawn filtered through the small window, casting long shadows across the room.

Lena was already awake, standing near the door, her face set in a determined expression. She was dressed and ready, her bag slung over her shoulder as she adjusted the gun holster at her waist. Her eyes met Alex's as he sat up, and she gave him a nod.

"It's time," she said simply.

Alex's muscles were stiff from the tension of the previous night, but he forced himself to stand, running a hand through his hair as he gathered his thoughts. They were about to dive deeper into the underworld of Kane's operation, and the stakes were higher than ever.

Lena handed him a small burner phone. "I've set up a secure line with my contact. He'll give us the details once we meet."

Alex took the phone, nodding as he slipped it into his pocket. His mind raced with the weight of what they were about to do. Veronica Lyons wasn't just any target—she was a key figure in Kane's empire, someone who could either be their salvation or their doom.

As they stepped out of the safe house and into the cold morning air, the city seemed to buzz with an electric tension. Every car that passed felt like a potential threat, every shadow a place for an enemy to hide. Alex could feel the pressure building in his chest as they moved through the quiet streets, the knowledge that they were being hunted gnawing at him with every step.

"We'll take the back streets," Lena said, her voice low. "Avoid the main roads. If Kane's men are looking for us, they'll be watching the usual routes."

Alex nodded, his pulse quickening as they moved deeper into the city's industrial district. The warehouses loomed ahead, their massive structures casting long shadows over the cracked pavement. It was a desolate place, the kind of area where people went to disappear—just the kind of place they needed for a secret meeting.

They reached the docks just as the sun began to rise, casting a pale orange glow over the water. The air smelled of salt and rust, the quiet hum of the port filling the stillness of the morning. Lena led the way to a large, rundown warehouse near the edge of the docks, her steps quick and purposeful.

As they approached the entrance, Alex's heart pounded in his chest. His mind raced with the possibilities of what lay ahead. Would this contact really help them? Or was this another trap, another piece of the deadly game Kane was playing?

Lena knocked twice on the rusted metal door, her hand hovering over the gun at her waist as they waited. The silence stretched on for what felt like an eternity, the tension in the air thick and suffocating.

Finally, the door creaked open.

A man stepped out, his face partially hidden by the shadow of the doorway. He was tall, with a lean, wiry frame and eyes that seemed to flicker with nervous energy. His gaze darted between Alex and Lena, sizing them up before he spoke.

"You Lena?" the man asked, his voice low and gravelly.

Lena nodded, her expression unreadable. "You're her contact?"

The man glanced over his shoulder before stepping aside to let them in. "Yeah. But we need to make this quick. Things are heating up. Kane's men have been sniffing around, and I don't want to be here when they show up."

Alex's stomach tightened at the mention of Kane's men, but he followed Lena inside. The warehouse was dark and musty, the air thick with the scent of old machinery and damp concrete. The man led them to a small office in the back, where the walls were lined with maps, photographs, and documents—evidence of Kane's sprawling network.

Lena crossed her arms, her eyes narrowing as she studied the man. "You said you had information on Veronica Lyons."

The man nodded, his eyes flicking toward the door again. "I do. But it's not good news."

Alex's heart sank at the man's words. He had been hoping for a lead, a way to track down Veronica and turn the tide in their favour. But the man's nervous energy and the way he kept glancing over his shoulder told Alex that something was wrong.

"She's disappeared," the man said quietly. "Vanished. No one's seen her in weeks."

Lena's jaw tightened, her hands balling into fists. "Where was she last seen?"

The man hesitated, his eyes flicking between them again. "Word on the street is she's gone underground. But there's a rumour—just a rumour—that she's still working for Kane. He's keeping her close."

Alex's stomach churned. If Veronica Lyons was still working for Kane, it would make their job infinitely harder. She knew how to cover her tracks, how to disappear when things got too hot. Finding her would be like chasing a ghost.

"We need to find her," Lena said, her voice hard. "If she's still working for Kane, she's the key to bringing him down."

The man shifted uncomfortably, his eyes darting toward the door again. "I can try to get more information, but it's risky. Kane's got eyes everywhere."

Lena stepped closer, her expression cold and determined. "Do it. We need to find her, and we need to do it fast."

The man swallowed hard, nodding quickly. "I'll do what I can. But be careful. Kane's already got men out looking for you. You're running out of time."

Alex's pulse quickened at the man's words. They were running out of time. Kane was closing in, and every move they made was being watched.

"We'll be ready," Lena said, her voice steady. "But we need that information."

The man gave a quick nod before slipping out the door, leaving Alex and Lena alone in the dimly lit office.

For a long moment, neither of them spoke, the weight of the situation pressing down on them like a heavy shroud. They were running out of options, and the longer it took to find Veronica Lyons, the closer Kane got to wiping them out.

"We'll find her," Lena said finally, her voice filled with quiet determination. "We have to."

Alex nodded, though the knot of anxiety in his chest didn't loosen. They were walking a razor's edge, and one wrong move could send them spiralling into the abyss.

But they didn't have a choice. The only way out of this was through Kane—and they would have to fight with everything they had to survive.

Chapter 22

Into the Depths

The low hum of the city buzzed faintly outside the warehouse, the distant sounds of traffic and the occasional clatter of machinery filling the early morning air. Inside the dimly lit office, Alex stood by the window, his eyes fixed on the shadows that clung to the alleyway just beyond the cracked glass. His thoughts were a mess of worry and anticipation, the weight of the mission pressing down on him like a heavy shroud. The meeting with Lena's contact had been both promising and ominous—a possible lead on Veronica Lyons, but no concrete answers, just more uncertainty.

He glanced back at Lena, who was pacing in the corner, her steps quick and tense. Her jaw was set, her eyes dark with concentration as she processed the information they had received. There was no doubt now—Kane's men were closing in, and their time was running out. Every second spent waiting was another opportunity for Kane to find them, another chance for him to silence them before they could make their next move.

"We need to move fast," Lena muttered, more to herself than to Alex. "If Veronica is still working for Kane, she'll know exactly where to hide. She's not going to make it easy for us."

Alex nodded, though the knot of anxiety in his chest had tightened even further. Veronica Lyons was their best chance at bringing down Kane, but she was also one of the most dangerous people in his orbit. If they found her, there was no guarantee that she would cooperate. And even if she did, they would be walking into a web of danger far more intricate than they could anticipate.

"Do you think she'll turn on Kane?" Alex asked, his voice low.

Lena paused, her gaze hardening as she considered his question. "Maybe. Veronica is loyal to Kane, but she's also smart. If she thinks he's going down, she might decide to save herself."

Alex's mind raced. They needed someone like Veronica—someone with the inside knowledge to dismantle Kane's empire from within. But getting her to turn on Kane would be a monumental task. She had been with him for years, and loyalty that deep wouldn't be easy to break.

"We'll have to offer her something," Lena said, crossing her arms. "Something that makes it worth the risk."

Alex frowned. "Like what?"

Lena leaned against the wall, her expression unreadable. "Protection. A way out. If we can convince her that we have the resources to keep her safe, she might flip."

Alex's stomach churned at the thought. The idea of making deals with someone like Veronica Lyons—a woman who had erased people from existence without a second thought—was unsettling. But they didn't have a choice. Kane was too powerful, too well-protected. They needed a key to unlock his empire, and Veronica was that key.

Lena pushed herself off the wall, her face set in determination. "We need to start tracking her down. My contact will get more information, but we can't sit around waiting. Every second counts."

Alex nodded, though the tension in his chest didn't ease. He glanced at the maps and photographs pinned to the walls, trying to piece together the puzzle that was Kane's network. They were walking blind, hoping that the next move wouldn't be their last.

They left the warehouse just as the sun was beginning to rise over the city, the first rays of light cutting through the dark, clouded sky. The industrial district was quiet, the streets almost deserted, but Alex couldn't shake the feeling that they were being watched. Every corner, every shadow felt like a potential threat, a place where Kane's men could be hiding, waiting for the perfect moment to strike.

Lena led the way, her steps quick and deliberate as they moved through the maze of alleys and side streets. They had to stay out of sight, had to stay one step ahead of Kane's forces. The longer they stayed in one place, the more likely it was that they would be found.

"We'll head to the south side of the city," Lena said as they walked, her voice low but firm. "There's a network of people who work in the underground—smugglers, hackers, informants. If Veronica's still in the city, someone down there will know where she's hiding."

Alex's heart raced at the thought. The south side of the city was notorious for being a hub of illegal activity. It was a place where people went to disappear, where deals were made in the shadows, far away from the eyes of the law. It was also a place where Kane's influence ran deep.

"You really think someone down there will talk to us?" Alex asked, his voice tight with concern.

Lena shot him a glance, her expression unreadable. "People will talk for the right price."

Alex swallowed hard. This was the world they were operating in now—a world of secrets and deals, of betrayal and danger at every turn. They weren't just fighting Kane's men anymore. They were stepping into a darker, more dangerous realm, where trust was a commodity and survival was never guaranteed.

They reached a quiet, nondescript building on the outskirts of the industrial district, far from the prying eyes of the authorities. The front of the building was nothing more than a rundown bar, the windows covered in grime and the paint peeling from the walls. But Alex knew that appearances were deceiving. This was one of the many fronts for the underground network that Lena had mentioned.

Inside, the air was thick with the scent of cigarette smoke and stale beer. The dim lighting cast long shadows across the room, where a few scattered patrons sat hunched over their drinks, lost in their own worlds. No one looked up as Alex and Lena entered, but Alex could feel the weight of their gazes, the subtle shift in the air as they moved toward the back of the bar.

Lena led him to a narrow hallway at the rear of the building, where a heavy steel door stood half-hidden behind a faded curtain. She knocked twice, her movements quick and precise, and after a long pause, the door creaked open.

A man stood on the other side, his eyes cold and calculating as he looked them over. He was tall, with a lean build and a scar that ran down the side of his face, disappearing into the collar of his jacket. His expression was unreadable, but there was a dangerous edge to his presence, a subtle tension that made Alex's skin crawl.

"This better be important, Lena," the man said, his voice low and gravelly. "I'm not in the mood for games."

Lena didn't flinch. "I need information. On Veronica Lyons."

The man's expression shifted, a flicker of surprise crossing his face before it disappeared just as quickly. He leaned against the doorframe, crossing his arms as he studied Lena with narrowed eyes.

"That's a dangerous name to be throwing around," he said quietly. "You know how close she is to Kane."

Lena's jaw tightened, but she didn't back down. "We're not here for gossip. We need to find her."

The man raised an eyebrow, his gaze flicking to Alex for a moment before returning to Lena. "And why would I help you? Kane's not exactly someone I want to piss off."

Lena took a step closer, her voice low and dangerous. "Because you owe me."

The man's eyes darkened, and for a long moment, the tension between them was palpable. Alex's heart pounded in his chest as he watched the silent exchange, wondering just how deep Lena's connections ran in this world. Whoever this man was, he clearly wasn't someone to be taken lightly.

Finally, the man sighed, his expression shifting into something closer to resignation. "Fine. But this is the last favour, Lena. After this, we're done."

Lena gave a curt nod, and the man stepped aside, motioning for them to follow him deeper into the building. The hallway was narrow and dimly lit, the walls covered in peeling paint and old posters. It was the kind of place that made Alex's skin crawl, but he followed without hesitation, trusting that Lena knew what she was doing.

They reached a small office at the end of the hall, where the man motioned for them to sit. He pulled a folder from the cluttered desk, tossing it onto the table in front of them.

"That's all I've got on her," the man said, his voice flat. "Veronica's been laying low for the past few weeks. No one's seen her, but I've heard whispers. Word is, Kane's got her stashed away somewhere in the north end. Safe house, heavily guarded."

Lena opened the folder, scanning the contents quickly. It was sparse—just a few photographs, a couple of addresses, and a list of possible associates. But it was enough. It was a lead.

"Thank you," Lena said, her voice cold but polite.

The man gave her a long, measured look. "Be careful, Lena. Kane's got eyes everywhere. If he finds out you're looking for Veronica, it won't end well for you."

Lena didn't respond. She simply closed the folder, stood, and motioned for Alex to follow her out of the room.

As they stepped back out into the cold morning air, Alex could feel the weight of their next move pressing down on him. They had a lead now—a possible location for Veronica Lyons—but the danger had escalated. If Kane knew they were looking for her, they would be walking straight into a trap.

"Do you trust him?" Alex asked as they made their way back to the car, the folder clutched tightly in Lena's hand.

Lena glanced at him, her expression hard. "I trust that he doesn't want to be on Kane's bad side. But we're on our own now. No more favours."

Alex's chest tightened at her words. They were getting closer to their target, but the closer they got, the more dangerous the situation became. Veronica Lyons wasn't just another cog in Kane's machine. She was a key player, someone with the power to bring everything crashing down.

But they had to find her first.

"We need to move fast," Lena said as they reached the car. "If Kane finds out we're onto her, he'll disappear her for good."

Alex nodded, sliding into the passenger seat as Lena started the engine. The tension between them was thick, the weight of the mission pressing down on them like a heavy shroud. They were heading into uncharted territory now, and the margin for error was razor-thin.

As they drove through the quiet streets of the city, Alex couldn't shake the feeling that they were being watched. Every car that passed felt like a potential threat, every pedestrian a spy for Kane's network. The pressure was mounting, and the air was thick with the knowledge that they were running out of time.

"We'll find her," Lena said quietly, as if reading his thoughts. "We have to."

Alex swallowed hard, his pulse quickening as they neared the north end of the city. They were stepping into a lion's den, and there was no turning back.

Chapter 23

Closing the Distance

The city's north end was a maze of forgotten streets, lined with old factories and warehouses that had long since fallen into disrepair. It was the kind of place people avoided, the kind of place where things happened in the dark and no one asked questions. As Lena drove through the winding streets, her face set in a hard expression, Alex couldn't help but feel the weight of what they were about to do. They were heading deeper into Kane's territory, into the heart of his operation, and if anything went wrong, there would be no way out.

The sky above them was a dull gray, the morning light barely breaking through the thick clouds that hung low over the city. The air felt heavy, thick with tension, as if the city itself knew something dangerous was coming. Alex shifted in his seat, his mind racing with everything that had happened in the past few days. They had come so far, but now they were entering the most dangerous phase of their plan.

Lena had hardly spoken since they left the underground network, her eyes fixed on the road, her hands tight on the wheel. She was always calm, always controlled, but Alex could sense the tension beneath the surface. This mission was dangerous, more dangerous than any of their previous moves, and they both knew it.

"We need to be ready for anything," Lena said, breaking the silence. Her voice was low but steady, the calm before a storm. "Veronica might not cooperate. She might already know we're coming."

Alex nodded, though his stomach churned at the thought. Veronica Lyons was their only real chance at taking Kane down, but she was also a master of manipulation and control. If she chose to turn on them, they would be walking into a trap of their own making.

"She'll cooperate," Alex said, more to reassure himself than anything else. "She'll have to."

Lena glanced at him, her expression unreadable. "Don't underestimate her. She's been with Kane for a long time. She knows how to play the game."

The weight of her words sank in, and Alex's heart pounded in his chest. They were relying on a dangerous gamble—one that could either bring Kane's empire crashing down or destroy them both.

The car finally came to a stop at the end of a narrow alley, hidden from the main road by a row of old shipping containers. Ahead of them stood a large, rundown warehouse, its windows boarded up, its exterior covered in layers of grime and graffiti. It looked abandoned, but Alex knew better. This was where Veronica was hiding.

"This is it," Lena said quietly, cutting the engine.

Alex swallowed hard, his pulse quickening. "What's the plan?"

Lena turned to face him, her eyes sharp and focused. "We go in quietly. If she's in there, we get her to talk. If she's not, we regroup. Either way, we need to be out of here before Kane's men catch up."

Alex nodded, though the knot of anxiety in his chest didn't loosen. He reached into his jacket, feeling the cold weight of the gun tucked into the holster at his side. He hated carrying it, hated the thought of using it, but he knew that in this world, hesitation could be fatal.

Lena opened the door, stepping out into the cold morning air, her movements smooth and deliberate. Alex followed, his heart pounding in his chest as they moved toward the side entrance of the warehouse. The building loomed over them, its decaying structure casting long shadows across the alley.

Lena motioned for Alex to stay close as she approached the door, her hand hovering over the lock-picking tools she carried in her jacket. She worked quickly, the soft click of the tumblers falling into place barely audible in the stillness.

As Lena opened the door and slipped inside, Alex followed closely behind, his senses on high alert. The warehouse was cold, dark, and eerily quiet. Dust particles floated in the air, catching the faint light that streamed through the cracks in the boarded-up windows. The smell of damp concrete and rust lingered in the stale air, giving the place an abandoned feel, but Alex knew better. Somewhere in here, Veronica Lyons was hiding.

Each step they took echoed softly, their footsteps bouncing off the cavernous walls. The silence felt oppressive, the kind of silence that weighed down on you, making you hyper-aware of every breath, every movement. Alex's heart pounded louder with every second, his mind racing as he prepared for whatever they were about to face.

Lena moved with a predator's grace, her hand steady on the grip of her gun, her eyes scanning the shadows for any sign of movement. Alex followed her lead, his pulse quickening as they made their way deeper into the warehouse.

They came to a stairwell that led to a mezzanine level, the metal stairs rusted and creaking underfoot as they ascended. The tension in the air was thick, the weight of their decision pressing down on them with every step they took. There was no turning back now.

As they reached the top, Alex spotted a faint light spilling out from beneath a door at the far end of the walkway. Lena saw it too, and she motioned for Alex to stay low as they approached. The door was old, its wooden surface splintered and worn, but it was the only sign of life in the otherwise abandoned building.

Lena pressed her ear against the door, listening for any movement inside. Her brow furrowed in concentration, and for a moment, Alex could see the strain behind her calm exterior. She was always so composed, always so in control, but he knew the pressure was mounting for both of them.

After a few seconds, Lena straightened up and gave Alex a nod. She gripped the handle of the door and pushed it open with a soft creak, her gun raised and ready as they stepped inside.

The room beyond was small, dimly lit by a single desk lamp that cast long shadows over the walls. It was cluttered with boxes and old equipment, the remnants of whatever operations had once run out of the warehouse. But in the center of the room, sitting calmly at the desk, was Veronica Lyons.

She didn't look surprised to see them. In fact, there was a hint of amusement in her eyes as she leaned back in her chair, crossing her legs casually as if they were old acquaintances dropping by for a visit.

"Well, well," Veronica said, her voice smooth and dripping with sarcasm. "I was wondering when you two would show up."

Alex's heart skipped a beat. She had been expecting them.

Lena's expression hardened, but she didn't lower her gun. "We're not here for games, Veronica."

Veronica smiled, tilting her head slightly as she looked them over. "Of course not. You're here for something much bigger, aren't you? You're here to take down Marcus Kane."

Alex felt a chill run down his spine. How much did she know? How had she anticipated their move?

"You have information we need," Lena said, her voice cold and measured. "Information that could end Kane's empire."

Veronica's smile widened, but it didn't reach her eyes. "You really think you can end Marcus Kane? That man has built an empire so deep, so ingrained in this city, that even if you took out a few key players, the machine would keep running."

Lena's jaw tightened, but her gaze didn't waver. "We're not looking to take out a few players. We're looking to dismantle the entire operation. And we need you to help us do that."

For a moment, the room was thick with silence. Veronica studied them, her gaze sharp and calculating. Alex could see the wheels turning in her mind, the way she was weighing her options, deciding how much to reveal and how much to keep hidden.

"And why would I help you?" Veronica asked finally, leaning forward slightly. "What's in it for me?"

Alex's stomach tightened. This was the part Lena had warned him about. Veronica Lyons wasn't just going to hand over the keys to Kane's empire. She would want something in return, something big.

"We can protect you," Lena said, her voice steady. "We can give you a way out."

Veronica raised an eyebrow, her expression sceptical. "A way out? From Kane?" She let out a soft, bitter laugh. "There is no way out from Marcus Kane. You know that as well as I do."

Lena didn't flinch. "If you stay with him, you're going down with the ship. Kane is a sinking ship, Veronica. You're too smart not to see that. Help us, and you can disappear. You can start over."

Veronica's eyes flicked to Alex, as if searching for some sign of weakness, some reason not to believe them. Alex's pulse quickened as he held her gaze, the tension between them palpable.

"You think I haven't tried to get out before?" Veronica said quietly, her voice laced with bitterness. "You think I haven't seen what happens to the people who betray Kane? He finds them. He always finds them."

"He won't find you if you're with us," Alex said, surprising himself with the confidence in his voice.

Veronica studied him for a long moment, her expression unreadable. Finally, she leaned back in her chair, her eyes narrowing slightly. "And what makes you think you can protect me? What makes you any different from all the others who have tried and failed?"

Alex swallowed hard, the weight of her question pressing down on him. The truth was, they didn't know for sure if they could protect her. They were just two people, up against one of the most powerful men in the city. But they had come too far to turn back now.

"We have the evidence," Lena said, her voice cutting through the tension. "We have everything we need to take Kane down. But we need you to fill in the gaps. We need the key to his operation."

Veronica's eyes flicked to the file Lena was holding, and for a moment, Alex saw a flicker of something—fear, maybe, or recognition. She knew how much danger she was in, and she knew they were offering her the only lifeline she had left.

"Tell us where Kane's weak spot is," Lena pressed. "Tell us what we need to bring him down."

Veronica's smile faded, and for the first time since they had entered the room, her expression softened slightly. There was a weariness in her eyes now, a heaviness that hadn't been there before.

"He doesn't have a weak spot," Veronica said quietly, her voice barely above a whisper. "Not the kind you're looking for."

Alex's heart sank. If Kane didn't have a weak spot, if there was no way to dismantle his operation, then everything they had done—all the risks, all the danger—would have been for nothing.

"There's always a weak spot," Lena said, her voice firm. "We just need you to show us where it is."

Veronica was silent for a long moment, her gaze drifting to the floor as if she was lost in thought. Finally, she let out a long breath and looked up at them.

"There's one way," she said softly. "But it's not what you think."

Alex's pulse quickened. "What is it?"

Veronica's eyes locked onto his, and the look in them made his stomach twist. "Kane doesn't have a weak spot because he's built his empire on fear. As long as people are afraid of him, as long as they believe he's untouchable, his power will never collapse."

"So how do we change that?" Lena asked, her voice steady.

Veronica's gaze flicked to the door, her expression darkening. "You have to take away his fear. You have to show people that he can be beaten."

The weight of her words settled over them like a heavy shroud. This wasn't just about finding one piece of information or one vulnerable part of Kane's empire. This was about dismantling the very foundation of his power—the fear that kept everyone under his control.

"And how do we do that?" Alex asked, his voice barely above a whisper.

Veronica's eyes narrowed. "You have to go after him directly. You have to hit him where it hurts. You have to make him bleed."

Chapter 24

The Price of Power

Veronica's words hung in the air like a heavy cloud, wrapping the room in a thick tension that made it difficult to breathe. Alex felt his pulse racing, his mind reeling from the weight of what she had just said.

"You have to go after him directly. You have to make him bleed."

The simplicity of it struck a chord, but it wasn't as simple as it sounded. Marcus Kane had built an empire of power, wealth, and control over decades. Striking at him directly meant putting themselves in the crosshairs of the most dangerous man in the city, and they both knew that once they started down this path, there would be no turning back.

Alex exchanged a glance with Lena, who was standing rigid by the door, her face unreadable. She had always been calm in the face of danger, but even now, Alex could see the toll this fight was taking on her. They had been running for so long—dodging death, betrayal, and heartbreak—and now they were about to face the greatest threat of all.

Lena took a step forward, her eyes locking onto Veronica's. "If we go after Kane, we need more than just advice on fear. We need leverage. Something concrete. We need to know his movements, his weaknesses. Where is he vulnerable?"

Veronica leaned back in her chair, her fingers lightly tapping the edge of the desk. For a moment, she seemed to be considering her options, weighing the risks of what she was about to reveal. Alex could see the flicker of hesitation in her eyes, the weariness of someone who had spent years working for a man like Kane. She was afraid, but she also knew this was her last chance.

"There's a facility," Veronica said finally, her voice low. "It's hidden deep in the outskirts of the city. Kane keeps it off the books—no official records, no traceable transactions. But it's where he stores everything. The real power of his empire. Documents, blackmail files, money laundering operations, and recordings. It's all there."

Alex felt his heart leap at the thought. This was what they needed—the key to dismantling Kane's entire empire. If they could get their hands on those files, they could expose everything. The corruption, the dirty deals, the lives ruined by Kane's grip on the city.

Lena's eyes narrowed. "Where is it?"

Veronica hesitated again, her gaze flicking toward the window as if she expected someone to be watching them, even here in the abandoned warehouse. She leaned in closer, lowering her voice to a whisper.

"It's on the outskirts, buried beneath an old manufacturing plant. Kane runs it through a shell corporation, but it's heavily guarded. You'll need more than just luck to get in."

Alex's stomach tightened at her words. Of course, it would be heavily guarded. Kane wasn't a fool. He knew how important those files were to maintaining his control. Breaking into that facility would be suicide if they didn't have a solid plan.

"We're going to need help," Alex said, his mind already spinning with possibilities. They couldn't do this alone. Not anymore. They would need to find someone who could help them penetrate Kane's defenses.

Lena nodded, already thinking ahead. "We'll reach out to Elena Vasquez. She'll have the connections we need to pull this off."

Veronica's expression darkened slightly at the mention of Elena's name. "Be careful with her. Kane's been gunning for her for years. If she gets caught in this, she's as good as dead."

"We all are," Lena replied coldly, her eyes flicking to Alex. "But we don't have a choice."

The tension in the room was palpable, and Alex could feel the weight of the decision pressing down on him. They were about to take the final step in their fight against Kane, but the risks had never been higher. This wasn't just about survival anymore. This was about taking down an entire empire, and they both knew that the consequences could be devastating.

Veronica stood slowly, walking over to the window and looking out at the crumbling cityscape beyond. Her shoulders sagged slightly, the weariness of her years working in the shadows evident in her posture.

"If you go after Kane," she said softly, almost to herself, "you better make sure you finish it. Because if you fail, there won't be anything left of you."

Lena's jaw clenched, but she didn't say anything. She didn't need to. They all knew the stakes.

Alex took a deep breath, trying to calm the storm raging inside him. His thoughts kept drifting back to Emily, still recovering in that clinic, unaware of the danger they were all in. She had been caught in the crossfire because of him, and if they didn't end this soon, she would be caught in it again. And next time, there wouldn't be a way out.

"We're going to need to move fast," Lena said, turning back toward the door. "Kane's not going to sit around waiting for us to make the first move."

Veronica didn't turn around, but her voice was cold and steady as she replied. "He's already moving. You're just trying to catch up."

The drive back to their temporary safe house was silent, the tension between Alex and Lena growing with each passing mile. Neither of them spoke, both lost in their own thoughts as the weight of their decision settled over them. The city passed by in a blur of lights and shadows, but Alex couldn't focus on anything beyond the growing sense of dread building inside him.

They were about to launch the most dangerous attack they had ever attempted. And they knew, deep down, that not all of them would survive it.

Lena pulled the car into a narrow alley behind a rundown apartment building, cutting the engine and sitting in silence for a moment before finally turning to face Alex. Her eyes were hard, but there was a flicker of something softer beneath the surface—something that looked like fear.

"We're running out of time," she said quietly. "If we don't hit Kane soon, he's going to find us."

Alex nodded, though the words felt hollow in his throat. "We'll need to get Elena involved. She'll have the contacts to help us breach the facility."

Lena hesitated for a moment, as if weighing her options. Then, with a resigned sigh, she reached for her phone. "I'll set up a meeting with her."

Alex's pulse quickened as Lena began typing a message to Elena. They were taking the next step, and there was no going back now. If they were going to survive this, they needed to hit Kane where it hurt—hard and fast.

As Lena sent the message, Alex leaned back in his seat, closing his eyes for a moment to steady himself. The exhaustion of the past few weeks was beginning to catch up with him, the constant fear and adrenaline taking its toll. But he couldn't rest. Not yet. Not until Kane was taken down.

"I don't know if we can trust her," Lena said suddenly, her voice breaking through Alex's thoughts.

He opened his eyes, turning to look at her. "Elena?"

Lena nodded, her expression guarded. "She's been trying to take Kane down for years, but she's been burned too many times. She might be willing to help us, but she's also going to be watching her own back."

Alex sighed, running a hand through his hair. "We don't have a choice. If we're going to hit that facility, we need her contacts."

Lena didn't respond right away, but Alex could see the conflict in her eyes. She was right to be cautious. They had been betrayed before—by people they thought they could trust. But Elena was their only option now. Without her help, they wouldn't stand a chance against Kane's defenses.

The phone buzzed in Lena's hand, and she glanced down at the screen. "She'll meet us in two hours."

Alex's heart skipped a beat. This was it. They were moving forward, and the final pieces of their plan were falling into place. But the dread in his chest only grew stronger.

As they stepped out of the car and made their way into the apartment building, Alex couldn't shake the feeling that this was the beginning of the end. The calm before the storm.

And when the storm hit, nothing would ever be the same.

Two hours later, Alex and Lena sat in the back corner of a small, dimly lit café on the outskirts of the city, their eyes scanning the entrance as they waited for Elena Vasquez to arrive. The tension between them was palpable, the weight of what they were about to do hanging over them like a dark cloud.

Elena had always been a wildcard in their plan—a woman with connections in both the legal and underground worlds, someone who had the resources to help them but also someone who had been burned by Kane too many times. Trusting her was a gamble, but they had no other choice.

The door to the café swung open, and Alex's heart skipped a beat as Elena stepped inside. She was dressed in her usual sharp, business-like attire, her dark hair pulled back into a sleek ponytail. Her eyes scanned the room before locking onto Alex and Lena, and she made her way over to them with quick, purposeful strides.

"You two are making a lot of noise," Elena said by way of greeting as she slid into the seat across from them. Her voice was calm, but there was a sharpness to her gaze that made Alex's skin prickle.

"We don't have time to be quiet," Lena replied, her voice steady. "We need your help."

Elena raised an eyebrow, leaning back in her chair. "You've never needed my help before. What's changed?"

Alex felt Lena tense beside him, but she didn't flinch. "We have a location. A facility where Kane keeps everything—his blackmail files, his money laundering operations, all of it. We're going to take it down."

Elena's eyes widened slightly, but she quickly masked her surprise. "That's a tall order."

"We can do it," Alex said, leaning forward. "But we need your contacts to get inside."

Elena was silent for a moment, her eyes narrowing as she studied them. Finally, she let out a soft sigh and shook her head. "You two have a death wish."

Lena didn't respond, but her eyes were hard as she met Elena's gaze. "Are you in or not?"

Elena smirked, leaning forward slightly. "I'm in. But you better be ready for what comes next. Because once we go after Kane, there's no going back."

Chapter 25

Into the Fire

The atmosphere inside Elena's small, dimly lit office felt thick, suffocating even, as if the air itself was aware of the storm about to break. Papers were spread across the table, maps of Kane's facility, hand-drawn diagrams of its security measures, and notes scribbled in hurried handwriting. The room was crowded with the weight of the task ahead, and Alex could feel the tension mounting between them as they reviewed the plan one last time.

Elena leaned over the table, her finger tracing the outlines of the facility's layout. "The perimeter is surrounded by private security, but Kane keeps it quiet—no uniforms, no overt signs of protection. Everything looks like an abandoned industrial plant on the outside. But once you get inside, it's a different story."

Alex studied the map, his pulse quickening as Elena pointed to the entrance. "Here," she continued, "is where you'll make your entry. The front is too heavily guarded, but the northwest side has a service tunnel used for maintenance. It's less visible and less patrolled. That's your way in."

Lena nodded, her gaze fixed on the diagrams as she absorbed every detail. Her focus was unwavering, but Alex could sense the tension radiating off her. This mission was more dangerous than anything they'd attempted before. One mistake, and they wouldn't make it out alive.

"What about inside?" Alex asked, his voice tight with anticipation. "How much resistance are we expecting?"

Elena's expression darkened as she glanced up from the map. "Once you're in, you'll have to move fast. The facility's lower levels are where Kane keeps his most important files—the blackmail material, the financial records, everything that can take him down. But those levels are also heavily secured. You'll need to disable the surveillance system before you can access them. I've got a contact who's provided a way to disrupt the cameras and alarms, but you'll only have a small window. After that, the system will reboot, and if you're still in there, you'll be trapped."

Alex's heart pounded in his chest. He could feel the gravity of Elena's words pressing down on him, the understanding that this mission wasn't just a strike against Kane—it was an all-or-nothing gamble. If they failed, they wouldn't get a second chance.

"We're going to need more than just speed," Lena said quietly, her eyes never leaving the map. "We'll need precision. This can't turn into a firefight."

Elena nodded, her face grim. "If it does, you're as good as dead. Kane's private security may not look like much on the outside, but they're well-trained, ex-military types. And if things get loud, reinforcements will be there in minutes."

Alex swallowed hard, the knot of anxiety tightening in his stomach. The risks were higher than ever, but this was their chance—the only chance—to bring Kane down. The files hidden in that facility were the key to dismantling his entire operation, to exposing the corruption that had allowed him to hold the city in his grip for so long. If they could get those files, everything would change.

"How do we get out?" Alex asked, glancing between Lena and Elena.

Elena tapped the map again, pointing to a secondary exit at the back of the facility. "Once you've got what you need, you'll exit through this service door. It leads to a tunnel that runs under the facility and opens up about two blocks away. It's the only way you'll be able to leave without drawing attention."

The silence that followed was thick with tension. They all knew the dangers, the slim margin for error. Alex's mind raced with the possibilities—what could go wrong, what they could face once inside. He had never felt the stakes this high before, not even during their escape from Hartman's safe house.

Lena finally straightened, folding her arms across her chest as she met Alex's gaze. "We're doing this. We've come too far to back down now."

Alex nodded, though his pulse pounded in his ears. He could see the determination in Lena's eyes, the same unrelenting drive that had kept them alive through every close call, every narrow escape. But this mission felt different—bigger, deadlier.

Elena glanced between them, her expression softening just slightly. "Once you're in, you're on your own. I'll be monitoring from here, but I won't be able to do much if things go sideways."

"They won't," Lena said firmly. "We'll get in, get the files, and get out."

But the weight of uncertainty still hung in the air. Even with the plan in place, there were too many variables, too many unknowns. And Kane wasn't the kind of man who left things to chance.

As the sun dipped below the horizon, casting the city in shadows, Alex and Lena found themselves standing on the roof of the rundown apartment building that had served as their temporary refuge. The distant hum of the city's streets seemed quieter now, almost muffled, as if the city itself was holding its breath.

Alex leaned against the rusted railing, staring out over the darkened skyline, his mind racing with everything they were about to face. He could feel the tension building inside him, the anxiety that had been gnawing at him ever since they'd decided to go after Kane directly. The gravity of what they were about to do—breaking into the heart of Kane's operation, striking at the core of his empire—felt like a weight pressing down on his chest.

Lena stood a few feet away, her gaze fixed on the horizon, her body still and calm. She had always been the rock—the one who kept them moving forward, the one who never flinched in the face of danger. But even now, Alex could see the weariness in her eyes, the strain of carrying the burden of their survival for so long.

"You think we'll make it?" Alex asked, his voice quiet but laced with the weight of his fear.

Lena didn't answer right away. Instead, she continued staring out at the city, her expression unreadable. After a long pause, she turned to face him, her eyes hard but softened by something unspoken.

"We don't have a choice," she said, her voice steady. "We either make it, or we die trying."

Alex's chest tightened at her words, the stark reality of their situation hitting him like a punch to the gut. There was no backup plan, no safety net. This mission was all or nothing.

"I don't want to lose you," Alex admitted, his voice barely above a whisper.

Lena's gaze softened just slightly, and for a moment, Alex saw the vulnerability she so rarely allowed herself to show. She stepped closer to him, her eyes never leaving his.

"You won't," she said quietly. "Not if we stick together."

The silence between them was heavy, charged with the weight of everything they had been through and everything they still had to face. Alex wanted to believe her, wanted to believe that they would come out of this alive, but the nagging voice in the back of his mind kept reminding him of the danger they were walking into.

He reached out, taking her hand in his. It was a small gesture, but in that moment, it felt like the only thing grounding him in the chaos of the world they were about to enter. Lena squeezed his hand, her grip firm and steady, as if she were silently reminding him that they were in this together.

"We'll get through this," she said, her voice filled with quiet resolve. "We always do."

But the truth was, Alex wasn't sure if they would. Kane was more dangerous than anyone they had ever faced. And the closer they got to taking him down, the more dangerous he became.

As the night deepened, they gathered their gear and reviewed the plan one final time. Alex's hands trembled slightly as he checked his gun, the cold metal feeling foreign in his grip. He wasn't a fighter, not like Lena, but he knew he had to be ready for anything. They were walking into enemy territory, and hesitation could mean death.

Lena packed her bag with precision, her movements quick and efficient as she prepared for the mission. She checked the black-out devices, the tools they would need to disable Kane's security system, and the small explosives they had brought in case things went south. Everything was methodical, every action deliberate.

"We move fast, stay quiet," Lena said, her voice low as they made their way down the narrow staircase of the apartment building. "We don't engage unless we have to."

Alex nodded, his pulse racing as they stepped out into the night. The air was cold, crisp, and the streets were eerily quiet. It was as if the city itself knew that something dangerous was about to happen.

They reached the car, and Lena slid into the driver's seat, her face set in hard determination. Alex followed, his heart pounding in his chest as they pulled away from the curb, the city lights fading into the distance as they headed toward the outskirts. Toward Kane.

The drive was silent, the tension between them thick as they approached the industrial district where Kane's facility was hidden. Alex's mind raced with the possibilities—what could go wrong, what they might face once inside. But no matter how many times he ran through the plan in his head, the knot of fear in his chest didn't loosen.

As they neared the facility, Lena slowed the car, pulling off the road into a darkened alley hidden from view. The factory loomed ahead, a massive structure surrounded by high walls and thick layers of security. It looked abandoned on the surface, but they both knew what lay beneath. This was the heart of Kane's empire.

Lena killed the engine, her eyes scanning the perimeter as she reached for her bag. "This is it," she said quietly, her voice steady despite the weight of what they were about to do.

Alex swallowed hard, his palms sweating as he gripped the handle of the car door. The adrenaline was already kicking in, his heart racing with a mix of fear and determination. This was the moment. Everything they had done—every risk, every close call—had led them here.

Lena opened her door and stepped out, moving quickly toward the edge of the wall that surrounded the facility. Alex followed, his breath coming in shallow bursts as they reached the hidden service tunnel that would lead them inside. Lena disabled the lock with practiced ease, and within moments, they were inside.

The tunnel was dark, damp, and smelled faintly of rust and oil. The only sound was the faint echo of their footsteps as they moved deeper into the facility, the weight of what they were about to do pressing down on them with every step.

Alex's heart pounded in his chest as they neared the end of the tunnel, the glow of dim lights just visible through the cracks in the door ahead. This was it—the point of no return.

Lena stopped, turning to face Alex, her expression unreadable in the shadows. "Ready?" she asked quietly.

Alex swallowed hard, nodding even though he wasn't sure if he really was.

With one last glance, Lena pushed open the door, and they stepped into the heart of Marcus Kane's empire.

Chapter 27

Hunted

The world felt like it was spinning out of control. Alex's lungs burned with every breath as he and Lena pushed through the narrow tunnel, the echo of the explosion still ringing in his ears. His legs felt like lead, each step an effort to keep moving, to keep running. But he couldn't stop. Not now. Not when they were so close. **Chapter 26**

Walking the Razor's Edge

The air inside Marcus Kane's facility was cold, sterile, and filled with a faint hum of electricity that seemed to echo through the walls. The corridor ahead was dimly lit, casting long shadows that danced across the concrete floor. Alex's heart pounded in his chest as he followed closely behind Lena, his eyes scanning every inch of their surroundings. This place felt like a labyrinth, a maze designed to swallow anyone who dared enter.

The door they had come through sealed behind them with a soft, metallic click, locking them into the heart of the beast. There was no turning back now.

Lena moved with a predator's grace, her footsteps light and soundless as she led the way deeper into the facility. Her face was set in hard determination, her eyes scanning every corner for signs of movement. Alex followed, gripping the black-out device in his hand, ready to disable the security systems when they reached the control room. They had a plan—a meticulous one—but the weight of its fragility pressed down on them both.

"Stay close," Lena whispered, her voice barely audible in the silence.

Alex nodded, though his breath came in shallow bursts. Every fiber of his being was on high alert, his senses heightened by the knowledge that they were walking into enemy territory. Kane's men could be anywhere, watching, waiting.

The facility was bigger than Alex had imagined. They passed through a series of narrow hallways, each one identical to the last, the walls lined with thick pipes and industrial equipment that hummed faintly with the pulse of power running through the building. It was a place that felt alive, as if the very walls were breathing, watching their every move.

"We need to find the security hub," Lena murmured, glancing back at Alex as they reached a junction. "Once we shut down the cameras, we can move more freely."

Alex's hands tightened around the black-out device, his nerves buzzing with anticipation. The thought of disabling Kane's security gave him a momentary sense of control, a brief illusion of power in a place where they had none. But he knew it wouldn't last. This facility was more than just a building—it was the nerve center of Kane's empire. And they were ants in a nest of predators.

Lena led the way to a narrow set of stairs, descending deeper into the facility. The air grew colder as they moved lower, the walls narrowing until the space felt claustrophobic, as though they were walking into the belly of a machine.

At the bottom of the stairs, they reached a door with a heavy electronic lock. Lena crouched down, her fingers moving quickly over the keypad as she worked to bypass the system. Alex stood behind her, his pulse racing as the minutes ticked by.

The silence felt oppressive, like a hand squeezing his throat, but Lena's calm focus gave him a thread of hope to cling to. She had gotten them this far—she would get them through this. She had to.

After a tense few seconds, the lock gave a soft click, and the door swung open with a low creak. Lena stood and motioned for Alex to follow. The room beyond was dark, but Alex could make out the faint glow of monitors lining the far wall.

"This is it," Lena whispered, stepping inside.

The control room was small, but it was packed with equipment—rows of screens displaying various sections of the facility, all being watched by unseen eyes. This was Kane's eye on his empire, the control hub that kept his secrets safe.

Lena moved quickly, scanning the consoles for the right system. "Once we shut down the cameras, we'll have five, maybe ten minutes before the security protocols kick back in. We'll need to move fast."

Alex nodded, his throat dry as he handed Lena the black-out device. "You're sure this will work?"

Lena's eyes flicked up to meet his, and for a moment, he saw the strain behind her steely exterior. "It has to."

She worked quickly, attaching the device to the main console and activating the signal. The hum of the monitors flickered briefly, and then, one by one, the screens went black. Alex's heart leapt in his chest. They had done it. For the first time since they'd entered the facility, they had the upper hand.

"Let's go," Lena said, her voice tight with urgency. "We've got a small window to reach the lower levels and find the files."

They left the control room quickly, moving with purpose through the darkened corridors. The facility was eerily silent now, the absence of the camera hum making every step feel louder, more dangerous. Alex's pulse raced as they descended deeper into the facility, the weight of what they were about to find pressing down on him like a lead blanket.

The lower levels of the facility were colder, more sterile, as if they had entered a different world entirely. The walls were bare, no longer lined with the machinery and pipes of the upper floors. This was where Kane kept his most valuable assets—the files that could expose everything.

They reached a large metal door at the end of the hall, sealed with a series of electronic locks and biometric scanners. Lena paused in front of it, her eyes narrowing as she examined the system.

"This is it," she whispered. "The vault."

Alex felt his stomach churn at the sight of the door. Whatever was behind it would be the key to bringing Kane down, but it would also put them in more danger than they had ever faced. Once they had the files, Kane would know. And he would come for them.

Lena pulled out the hacking device Elena had given them, attaching it to the biometric scanner. The seconds ticked by in agonizing silence as the device worked its way through the system. Alex could feel his heart pounding in his ears, the anticipation building like a storm about to break.

Then, with a soft beep, the lock disengaged, and the door slid open.

Lena stepped inside first, her eyes scanning the room. The vault was massive, filled with rows of metal shelves lined with boxes, folders, and digital drives. It was a treasure trove of information—Kane's entire empire, cataloged and stored for safekeeping.

"We don't have much time," Lena said, her voice low but urgent. "Start looking for anything related to his blackmail operations and financial records."

Alex moved quickly, his hands shaking as he rifled through the shelves. Each folder he opened was filled with documents detailing bribes, political favours, and dirty deals that stretched back decades. It was overwhelming—more corruption than he had ever imagined. This was the evidence that could topple Kane's empire.

But as the minutes ticked by, the unease in Alex's chest grew. They had been here too long. The cameras would be back online soon, and the security systems would reboot. If they didn't move fast, they would be trapped.

"I've got something," Lena said, pulling a thick folder from one of the shelves. Her eyes were wide as she scanned the contents. "These are the financial records. This is what we need."

Alex felt a wave of relief wash over him. They had it—the key to bringing Kane down. But that relief was short-lived. The sound of footsteps echoed from the corridor outside, growing louder with each passing second.

Lena's eyes snapped up, her body tensing. "We need to go. Now."

Alex stuffed the folder into his bag, his heart pounding as the footsteps grew closer. They had been found. There was no time to think, no time to plan. They had to run.

The corridor outside was a blur of shadows as Alex and Lena sprinted down the hall, the sound of approaching guards chasing them like a dark cloud. The adrenaline pumping through Alex's veins blurred his vision, but all he could think about was the folder in his bag. They had the evidence, but they needed to get out. Fast.

"Go left!" Lena shouted as they reached a junction, her voice barely audible over the pounding of their feet.

They turned sharply, their footsteps echoing off the concrete walls. Alex's lungs burned as he pushed himself harder, his heart hammering in his chest. The facility's security system was back online, and the guards were closing in. They wouldn't have much time before the entire place was swarming with Kane's men.

"We're almost there!" Lena called, her voice strained.

The service tunnel was just ahead. If they could reach it, they might have a chance to escape. But as they rounded the final corner, Alex's heart sank.

A group of guards stood between them and the exit, their weapons drawn, their eyes cold and calculating.

"Drop the bags!" one of the guards shouted, his voice sharp and commanding.

Alex froze, his chest heaving as the reality of the situation sank in. They were trapped. The guards had them cornered, and there was no way out.

Lena's eyes darted to Alex, her face pale but determined. She didn't say anything, but Alex could see the decision in her eyes. They weren't going to surrender. Not now.

Before he could react, Lena moved. Fast. Her hand shot to the small explosives she had stashed in her bag, and in one fluid motion, she tossed them toward the guards.

"Run!" Lena shouted.

The explosion ripped through the corridor, the shockwave slamming into Alex like a freight train. He stumbled, his ears ringing as the dust and debris filled the air. The guards were disoriented, some knocked to the ground, others scrambling to recover.

"Come on!" Lena shouted, grabbing Alex's arm and pulling him toward the tunnel.

They ran, their bodies aching, their lungs burning as they pushed through the smoke and chaos. The exit was just ahead, the tunnel their only hope of escape.

But even as they reached the tunnel, Alex knew this was far from over. Kane would come for them. And the next time, there would be no escape.

Behind them, the sounds of shouts and footsteps echoed through the tunnel, growing louder with every second. Kane's men were right behind them, their boots pounding on the cold concrete as they chased Alex and Lena through the labyrinthine underground system. There was no room for error—no time to think. They had to keep moving, or they'd be caught.

"We're almost there," Lena panted, glancing back at Alex as they rounded another corner.

The tunnel twisted and turned in a disorienting pattern, but Lena knew the way. She had memorized the layout before they had entered the facility, and now it was their only hope of survival. Alex's mind raced, the weight of the evidence in his bag pressing down on him like a heavy burden. They had what they needed to take Kane down, but getting out alive was another story.

The tunnel finally opened up into a small exit, a rusted metal door that led out into the industrial district two blocks away from Kane's facility. Lena slammed her shoulder into the door, forcing it open with a loud creak. Cold air hit them like a slap to the face as they stumbled out into the night, the city lights barely visible through the fog.

Alex gasped for breath, his heart pounding in his chest as they staggered toward the nearest alley. His body ached from the exertion, every muscle screaming for rest, but they couldn't stop. Not yet. The danger was still too close.

"They'll be searching the area," Lena said, her voice tight with urgency. "We need to get off the streets."

Alex nodded, barely able to form words through the exhaustion. His mind was spinning, the adrenaline still coursing through his veins as they ducked into the shadows of the alley. They had to disappear, blend into the city's underbelly before Kane's men could track them down. But the question gnawed at him: how long could they keep running?

"We need to contact Elena," Alex managed to say between gasps of air. "She has to know we got the files."

Lena's face was set in hard determination as she checked the small burner phone she had been carrying. "No signal here. We'll need to move a few blocks before we can call her."

Alex's heart sank. They weren't out of the woods yet. Every moment they spent exposed on the streets was a moment Kane's men could close in on them. But they didn't have a choice. They had to get to a safe spot—fast.

They stuck to the shadows as they moved through the industrial district, weaving through alleyways and abandoned buildings, staying out of sight. The sounds of sirens in the distance filled the air, but Alex couldn't tell if they were for them or just the normal hum of the city's chaos. Every noise felt like a threat, every shadow like a potential enemy.

Lena stopped at a street corner, peering out from behind a rusted fence as she scanned the area. "This way," she whispered, motioning for Alex to follow.

They slipped into another alley, this one narrower and darker than the last. The tension between them was palpable, the silence filled with unspoken fears. Alex's mind raced with thoughts of what would happen next. They had the evidence, but what if Kane already knew? What if they were being watched, even now?

Lena paused, pulling out the burner phone again. She pressed a few buttons, her face tense as she waited for the call to connect.

"Elena," she whispered sharply. "We got the files. But Kane's men are all over us. We need extraction."

There was a long pause, and Alex felt his heart tighten in his chest as he watched Lena's expression darken.

"What do you mean it's not safe?" Lena hissed, her voice barely controlled.

Alex's stomach dropped. Something was wrong.

"They're tightening their grip," Lena continued, her eyes narrowing as she listened to Elena's voice on the other end. "Damn it."

She ended the call abruptly, turning to Alex with a grim expression. "Kane's men are already swarming the area. Elena can't get to us without being compromised. We're on our own."

Alex's heart pounded in his chest, the reality of their situation sinking in like a heavy weight. They were alone, cut off from their only source of backup, and Kane's men were closing in. The folder in his bag felt heavier with every passing second, the evidence that could destroy Kane's empire now their only lifeline. But if they couldn't get out of the city, none of it would matter.

"What do we do?" Alex asked, his voice tight with fear.

Lena's jaw clenched as she glanced around the alley, her mind clearly racing with options. "We need to lie low. Get somewhere Kane's men won't think to look."

Alex swallowed hard, his mind spinning with the possibilities. "Do you have a place in mind?"

Lena hesitated for a moment, her eyes narrowing as if weighing their options. Finally, she nodded. "There's a safe house I used a long time ago. It's not far from here, but it's risky."

"We don't have a choice," Alex said, his voice firmer than he expected.

Lena didn't argue. She motioned for Alex to follow her, and together they made their way deeper into the shadows of the city. The streets felt colder now, more menacing, as if the entire city was closing in around them. But Alex forced himself to focus on the task at hand. They had made it this far—they couldn't give up now.

The safe house Lena led them to was a nondescript building on the edge of the industrial district, hidden behind a row of old warehouses that had long since been abandoned. The windows were boarded up, the exterior covered in layers of grime and rust. It looked like any other forgotten building in this part of the city—exactly the kind of place no one would think to search.

Lena jimmied the lock with practiced ease, and the door swung open with a soft creak. Inside, the air was stale and cold, the faint smell of dust and mildew lingering in the shadows. It was dark, with only a few old pieces of furniture scattered across the small room.

"It's not much," Lena said quietly, closing the door behind them, "but it'll keep us hidden for a while."

Alex dropped his bag onto the floor, his entire body aching from the tension and exhaustion. The adrenaline that had been keeping him going was finally starting to wear off, leaving him feeling drained, both physically and mentally.

"We need to figure out our next move," Lena said, pacing the length of the room. "Kane's not going to stop until he finds us. We have the files, but getting them to the right people is going to be harder than we thought."

Alex ran a hand through his hair, his mind racing. "Can't we send them to the press? Make it public so Kane can't bury it?"

Lena shook her head, her expression grim. "It's not that simple. Kane has connections everywhere. If we send the files to the wrong person, they'll disappear before they ever see the light of day. We need to make sure they get into the hands of someone who can't be bought."

Alex's stomach churned at the thought. The files in his bag were powerful enough to take down an empire, but only if they could get them to the right people. And with Kane's men closing in, every second they spent hiding was another second they could be caught.

"We can't stay here forever," Alex said, glancing around the small room.

Lena nodded, her face set in hard determination. "I know. But we need to rest. Just for a few hours. We'll move again before sunrise."

Alex nodded, though the thought of resting seemed impossible with the weight of the situation pressing down on them. His mind was still spinning, the fear of being caught gnawing at the back of his thoughts. But he knew Lena was right. They couldn't keep running forever—not without a plan.

Lena moved to the small window, peering out through a crack in the boarded-up slats. "I'll take first watch. You try to get some sleep."

Alex hesitated, his body tense with the urge to keep moving, to stay alert. But his exhaustion finally won out, and he sank down onto the old, worn-out couch in the corner of the room. His body ached, his mind still buzzing with thoughts of what lay ahead. But for now, he had to trust Lena to keep them safe.

He closed his eyes, the weight of everything they had been through crashing down on him all at once. The sound of Lena's quiet footsteps pacing the room was the only thing that kept him grounded, reminding him that they weren't alone. Not yet.

But deep down, Alex knew that their time was running out. And when Kane found them, there would be no more hiding.

Chapter 28

Cornered

The silence inside the safe house was thick, oppressive. Alex lay on the worn-out couch, his eyes shut but his mind still spinning. Sleep was elusive, slipping away the moment he began to drift off. His body ached with exhaustion, every muscle sore from the adrenaline-fueled sprint through Kane's facility and the long hours of tension that followed. But rest didn't come easily, not when the weight of everything they were facing pressed down on him like a heavy blanket.

Somewhere across the room, Lena's quiet footsteps echoed as she paced back and forth, her form a dark silhouette against the faint glow of the boarded-up window. She hadn't spoken much since they'd arrived at the safe house. Her mind was always working, always one step ahead, but Alex could see the toll this was taking on her too. They had been running for so long, and now they were backed into a corner with nowhere else to go.

The files they had stolen from Kane's facility were their only hope, but even that hope was fragile. Getting the evidence into the right hands was proving harder than they'd expected, and every minute they spent hiding felt like another minute closer to being caught.

Alex opened his eyes, the dim light of the room casting long shadows across the cracked walls. His thoughts drifted to Emily, still recovering in that clinic, unaware of the danger that was closing in on all of them. Guilt gnawed at him, a constant presence in the back of his mind. If they failed, it wasn't just his life on the line—it was everyone he cared about.

He pushed himself up from the couch, wincing at the stiffness in his muscles, and glanced over at Lena. She stood by the window, her face partially hidden in the shadows, but Alex could see the hard lines of tension in her posture.

"You should rest," Alex said quietly, his voice rough from exhaustion.

Lena shook her head, not turning to face him. "We can't afford rest. Not now."

Alex sighed, running a hand through his hair. He understood the pressure Lena was under. She had carried them through every dangerous situation they'd faced, always keeping them one step ahead of Kane's men. But he could see the cracks forming. She was pushing herself to the brink, and if they didn't find a way out soon, it would be too late.

"Lena," Alex said softly, standing and moving closer to her. "We'll figure it out. But you need to rest. You can't keep running on fumes."

Lena's eyes flicked to him for a brief moment, the hardness in her expression softening just slightly. "I can rest when this is over," she muttered, turning her gaze back to the window.

Alex frowned, stepping beside her and glancing out through the narrow crack in the boarded-up window. The city outside was quiet, the streets deserted, but that only made the tension worse. The calm before the storm.

"We can't stay here much longer," Lena said, her voice low but steady. "Kane's men will eventually figure out where we are."

Alex nodded. He knew she was right. The safe house had provided them with a brief respite, but it wasn't enough. They needed to get the files out before Kane closed in on them. But every plan they had come up with so far had felt like a dead end.

"Elena can't help us," Alex said, frustration creeping into his voice. "Kane's got the city locked down."

Lena's jaw tightened, her eyes narrowing in thought. "There's still one option," she said after a long pause. "It's risky, but it might be the only way to get the files to someone who can actually do something with them."

Alex's pulse quickened as he glanced at her. "What are you thinking?"

Lena finally turned to face him, her eyes hard but determined. "There's an underground network—journalists, whistleblowers, people who've been fighting Kane from the shadows. They're off the grid, but I've worked with them before. If we can get the files to them, they'll know how to get it out without being intercepted."

Alex felt a spark of hope flicker in his chest. This was the first real plan they'd had since escaping the facility, but the mention of "risky" lingered in his mind. "How do we contact them?"

Lena's lips pressed into a thin line. "We don't. We go to them."

The night was cold, the air sharp and biting as Alex and Lena made their way through the darkened streets. They moved quickly, staying close to the shadows, every step measured and deliberate. The industrial district behind them had fallen into silence, but the weight of Kane's presence lingered, an invisible threat that loomed over them.

Alex's heart pounded in his chest as they navigated the narrow alleyways and deserted side streets, the tension between them growing with every step. Lena had explained the location of the underground group—a hidden base buried deep beneath the city, accessed through a series of tunnels that snaked through the old subway system. It was a place that had long since been abandoned by the city, forgotten by most, but it had become a safe haven for those fighting against Kane's influence.

As they moved, Alex couldn't shake the feeling that they were being watched. Every corner they turned, every shadow they passed, felt like a pair of eyes tracking their movements. He glanced at Lena, but her face remained impassive, her focus entirely on their mission. She was always like this—calm under pressure, never letting fear show—but Alex knew she felt it too. They were being hunted, and it was only a matter of time before Kane's men caught up.

The entrance to the underground network was hidden behind an old, rusted gate at the edge of the city's forgotten subway system. The tracks had long since been abandoned, the tunnels left to rot, but the group Lena had mentioned had turned it into a fortress of sorts. A place where they could continue their fight without fear of being found.

Lena knelt by the gate, her fingers working quickly to pick the lock. Alex kept watch, his body tense, every nerve on edge. The cold wind whipped through the empty streets, but the silence was the worst part. It made every small sound—every creak of metal, every rustle of leaves—seem amplified, like a threat waiting just beyond the shadows.

The lock finally clicked, and Lena pushed the gate open, motioning for Alex to follow. They slipped inside, descending a narrow staircase that led into the depths of the old subway tunnels. The air grew colder the further they went, the smell of damp concrete and rust filling the space around them.

Alex's heart pounded in his chest as they reached the bottom of the stairs, the darkness pressing in from all sides. The tunnels stretched out before them, a maze of twists and turns, each path leading deeper into the underground.

"Stay close," Lena whispered, her voice barely audible in the thick silence.

Alex nodded, his eyes scanning the darkened tunnel as they moved forward. The walls were covered in graffiti, old and faded, but the further they went, the more recent markings began to appear—symbols, warnings scrawled in hastily painted strokes. This wasn't just an abandoned tunnel. This was territory. The territory of people who didn't want to be found.

They moved deeper into the tunnels, the sound of their footsteps echoing off the walls. The tension was palpable, the weight of the underground pressing down on them. Alex could feel the anxiety gnawing at the edges of his mind, but he pushed it down, focusing on the task ahead. They had to reach the group. They had to deliver the files.

After what felt like hours, they reached a junction in the tunnel. Lena paused, her eyes narrowing as she scanned the walls, looking for something. Alex's heart raced as the silence stretched on, the darkness around them feeling more oppressive with each passing second.

Suddenly, a soft voice echoed from the shadows.

"Stop."

Alex's breath caught in his throat, his hand instinctively going to the gun at his side. He couldn't see where the voice had come from, but it was close—too close.

Lena's hand shot out, gripping his arm to keep him from drawing his weapon. "We're not here to fight," she said, her voice calm but firm. "We're here to talk."

A figure stepped out from the shadows, a tall, wiry man dressed in dark clothing, his face obscured by the hood of his jacket. His eyes glinted in the faint light, cold and calculating as they scanned Lena and Alex.

"Who sent you?" the man asked, his voice sharp.

"No one," Lena replied. "We're here to deliver something. Evidence. On Kane."

The man's eyes narrowed, his posture tense. "That's a dangerous name to throw around down here."

"We know," Lena said, her voice steady. "That's why we're here."

For a long moment, the man didn't move, his gaze flicking between Alex and Lena as if weighing their words. Then, without a word, he turned and motioned for them to follow.

The tunnels grew darker and more twisted as they followed the man deeper into the underground. The air was colder here, thick with moisture and the smell of rust and decay. But there was also something else—an energy that Alex couldn't quite place. This was a place of resistance, a place where people had come together to fight against the power that Kane wielded over the city.

They finally reached a large, open space—an old subway station that had been repurposed into a base of operations. The station was dimly lit by a few scattered lamps, and people moved quietly through the shadows, their faces hard and determined. Alex could see the makeshift command center set up in the middle of the station—old computers, maps pinned to the walls, and a flurry of activity as people worked to gather information.

"This is the place," the man said, stopping in front of the command center. "Talk to her."

Alex followed the man's gaze to a woman standing at the center of the room, her sharp eyes fixed on a series of maps. She was older, her face lined with years of experience, but there was an unmistakable fire in her gaze. She looked up as they approached, her eyes narrowing as she took in Lena and Alex.

"You've got something on Kane?" she asked, her voice direct.

Lena nodded, pulling the folder from her bag and handing it to the woman. "Everything. Financial records, blackmail material, details on his entire operation. It's enough to take him down."

The woman's eyes flicked to the folder, her expression unreadable. She opened it slowly, scanning the contents with a practiced eye. Alex held his breath, waiting for her reaction, the weight of their mission pressing down on him.

Finally, the woman looked up, her gaze hard but approving. "This is good. But it's not enough."

Alex's heart sank. "What do you mean?"

The woman's eyes flicked to him. "Kane's network runs deep. These files are a start, but if you want to take him down for good, you need more. You need someone on the inside."

Lena frowned. "We've already risked everything to get this. What more can we do?"

The woman's gaze sharpened. "There's someone in Kane's inner circle. Someone who's been looking for a way out. If you can get to him, he'll give you the last piece of the puzzle."

Alex's stomach tightened. This was getting more dangerous by the second. "Who is it?"

The woman's eyes met his, her voice steady and cold. "Detective Samuel Reed."

Chapter 29

Into The Lions Den

The name **Samuel Reed** hung in the air like a dark cloud, casting a shadow over the conversation. Alex felt a chill crawl down his spine. The mention of Reed brought up memories of tense encounters, of rumours whispered in the dark about a detective who played both sides of the law. A man who walked the line between justice and corruption.

"He's dangerous," Lena said, her voice tight with concern as she looked at the woman in charge of the underground network. "Reed isn't someone you just approach. He's loyal to Kane."

The woman, her eyes hardened by years of fighting the system, nodded but didn't flinch. "He's loyal because he thinks Kane is untouchable. But that's changed. Word on the street is that Reed is looking for a way out. He's seen what happens to those who cross Kane, and now he's trapped between two worlds."

Alex glanced at Lena, sensing her hesitation. He knew Reed's name, knew his reputation as a man who played by his own rules. But he also knew that Reed was the kind of person who could help them, or destroy everything they'd worked for.

"We don't have a choice," Alex said quietly, turning to face Lena. "If we don't get to Reed, Kane will stay one step ahead. We need him."

Lena's jaw clenched, her gaze hardening as she processed Alex's words. She didn't like it—neither did Alex—but they both knew the woman in front of them was right. Reed was their best shot at getting the last piece of the puzzle, the insider information they needed to expose Kane's empire from within.

"Where can we find him?" Lena finally asked, her voice flat but resigned.

The woman crossed her arms, her expression grim. "He's laying low right now. Ever since you two started making waves, Kane's been tightening his grip on anyone close to him. Reed's no exception. But there's a place in the city he frequents—quiet, off the radar. If you want to make contact, that's where you'll need to go."

Alex's stomach tightened as the woman handed Lena a slip of paper with an address scribbled on it. The location was in one of the city's more dangerous districts, a place known for its lawlessness, where Kane's influence ran deep. Going there would be like walking into the lion's den.

"Be careful," the woman warned. "Reed's not stupid. If he thinks you're setting him up, he'll kill you before you have a chance to explain."

Lena folded the paper and slipped it into her jacket. Her eyes met Alex's, and he could see the resolve behind her gaze. This was it—the next step in their mission to take Kane down. But the risks had never been higher.

"We'll get to him," Lena said, her voice filled with quiet determination. "And we'll make him talk."

The city looked different at night, especially in the part where Alex and Lena now found themselves. The narrow streets of the downtown district were shrouded in shadows, the flickering streetlights casting uneven patches of light across the broken pavement. The air was thick with the smell of garbage and gasoline, the sounds of distant sirens and muffled voices echoing through the alleyways.

They were deep in Kane's territory now. Every building, every corner was marked with his invisible fingerprints. The people who lived here knew better than to talk about it, but they all understood the truth—this part of the city belonged to Kane.

Alex's heart raced as they moved quietly through the maze of streets, their eyes scanning the shadows for any sign of danger. Lena led the way, her posture tense but composed, her hand hovering close to the gun tucked into her jacket. She was always alert, always ready for the worst, and Alex was grateful for her steady presence.

The address they'd been given led them to a dilapidated bar tucked away in the back of an alley, its windows dark, its neon sign flickering weakly in the night. The place looked like it hadn't seen a renovation in decades—exactly the kind of spot where a man like Reed would go to disappear.

"This is it," Lena whispered, stopping just before the entrance. "Stay sharp."

Alex nodded, his pulse quickening as they approached the door. They both knew how dangerous this was—approaching Reed without a clear plan was like poking a bear. But they were out of options. The files they'd stolen from Kane's facility were important, but without Reed's insider information, they weren't enough to dismantle Kane's entire operation.

Lena pushed the door open, and they stepped inside. The bar was small and dingy, the air thick with the smell of stale beer and cigarette smoke. A few patrons sat scattered around the room, hunched over their drinks, their faces hidden in the dim light. No one looked up as Alex and Lena entered, but the tension in the air was palpable.

"There," Lena whispered, nodding toward a corner table near the back of the room.

Alex's eyes followed her gaze, landing on a man sitting alone at the table, his back to the wall. He looked older than Alex had expected, his face lined with the weight of years spent navigating the dangerous waters of Kane's world. His clothes were plain, his expression unreadable as he nursed a glass of whiskey, but Alex recognized him instantly.

Detective Samuel Reed.

Lena motioned for Alex to stay close as they made their way toward the table. The dim light flickered above them, casting long shadows across the room as they approached. Reed didn't look up as they reached him, his eyes fixed on his drink, but Alex could feel the tension radiating off him. He knew they were there.

"We need to talk," Lena said quietly, standing just a few feet from the table.

Reed's eyes flicked up, his gaze cold and calculating as he looked at Lena, then at Alex. For a long moment, he didn't say anything. The air between them was thick with unspoken threats, the weight of the danger they were walking into pressing down on them like a vise.

Finally, Reed leaned back in his chair, his eyes narrowing. "You've got some nerve coming here."

Alex swallowed hard, his heart pounding in his chest. Reed's reputation was well-known, and now that they were standing in front of him, Alex could feel the full weight of that reputation. Reed was dangerous—maybe more dangerous than Kane's enforcers. He wasn't a man who could be intimidated or reasoned with easily.

"We didn't have a choice," Lena said, her voice steady despite the tension. "We need your help."

Reed raised an eyebrow, his expression darkening. "And why would I help you?"

Lena took a step closer, her eyes never leaving Reed's. "Because you want out. And we can give you that."

Reed's gaze flicked to Alex, and for a moment, the silence in the bar felt suffocating. Alex could see the gears turning in Reed's mind, the calculations he was making, weighing his options. This was a man who had spent his entire career playing both sides—working for the law and for men like Kane. He knew how to survive, and right now, Alex could see him trying to figure out if they were his way out.

"You don't know anything about me," Reed said finally, his voice low and dangerous.

Lena didn't flinch. "I know you're stuck. Kane's closing in, and you don't have a way out. But we do. You help us, and we'll take him down. You'll be free."

Reed leaned forward, his eyes narrowing as he studied Lena. "And what makes you think I want to be free?"

For the first time, Lena's expression softened, just slightly. "Because I know what it's like to be trapped. And I know you're too smart to think Kane will keep you around once he's done with you."

The silence stretched on, thick and heavy, as Reed continued to stare at Lena. Alex's heart pounded in his chest, his hands clenched into fists at his sides. This was it—the moment they either won Reed over or lost everything.

Finally, Reed let out a long sigh, running a hand through his graying hair. "You're asking for a lot," he muttered, glancing down at his drink. "You realize that, right?"

"We're asking for what you've been waiting for," Lena said softly. "A way out. A way to take Kane down."

Reed was silent for a long time, his fingers drumming on the edge of the table. Alex could feel the tension rising, the weight of the decision pressing down on all of them. If Reed agreed to help, they would have the final piece of the puzzle. If he refused, they were back to square one—and Kane would continue to hunt them.

Finally, Reed looked up, his eyes locking onto Lena's. "Alright," he said quietly. "But if I do this, I'm not doing it for you. I'm doing it for me."

Lena nodded, her expression unreadable. "That's all we need."

The air outside the bar was cold and biting as Alex and Lena stepped back into the narrow alley. The tension between them had lessened slightly, but the weight of what they had just accomplished still hung in the air. Reed had agreed to help them, but Alex knew it was a fragile alliance. Trusting Reed was like walking a tightrope, and one wrong move could send them all plummeting.

"We need to move fast," Lena said quietly, her eyes scanning the street as they made their way through the shadows. "Reed's information will be enough to take Kane down, but we don't have much time. If Kane gets wind of this, we're finished."

Alex nodded, his heart still racing from the intensity of their conversation with Reed. The man was dangerous—there was no doubt about that—but he was also their only chance at bringing down Kane's empire from the inside. And now, they had to make sure they used that chance wisely.

As they moved through the darkened streets, Alex couldn't shake the feeling that they were being watched. Every shadow seemed to move, every sound felt amplified. The fear that had been gnawing at him since they'd escaped Kane's facility was back, stronger than ever.

Lena glanced at him, her expression hard but filled with resolve. "We're close, Alex. We can end this."

Alex wanted to believe her. He wanted to believe that they were finally on the verge of bringing Kane's empire crashing down. But deep down, he knew that the hardest part was still ahead of them.

And with Kane's men closing in, there was no room for error.

Chapter 30

A Deal with the Devil

The cold air gnawed at Alex's skin as he and Lena moved quickly through the dark streets, the sound of their footsteps lost in the hum of the city's night. The meeting with Detective Samuel Reed had gone better than they had expected—he had agreed to help. But the price of that help hung heavy in the air, unspoken but palpable.

Reed wasn't doing this for them. He was doing it for himself. And that made him as much of a threat as he was an asset.

Lena's face was set in hard lines as they made their way through the narrow alleyways, her eyes constantly scanning for threats. They had to stay on the move, stay ahead of Kane's men. Now more than ever, they couldn't afford to be caught. Reed had provided them with crucial information, but they were walking on a knife's edge. One slip, one misstep, and it would all be over.

"We need to talk," Lena said quietly, breaking the silence as they neared their temporary safe house.

Alex nodded, though his mind was still spinning from the intensity of their meeting with Reed. Trusting him felt like playing Russian roulette. At any moment, the man could decide to turn on them, and there would be no way to stop him. But they didn't have a choice. Without Reed's insider knowledge, they would never be able to dismantle Kane's empire.

Once inside the safe house—a rundown apartment building tucked away on the outskirts of the city—Lena paced the small room, her frustration evident in every movement. She was wound tight, the pressure of their situation weighing heavily on her shoulders. Alex watched her, his heart pounding in his chest as he tried to process everything they had just learned.

Reed had given them a way in, but it wasn't going to be easy. The final steps of their plan involved getting deeper into Kane's operation than they had ever dared before. And the risks were greater than anything they had faced.

"Do you trust him?" Alex asked, breaking the heavy silence.

Lena stopped pacing, her eyes flicking to Alex. For a moment, she didn't answer. She didn't need to. The doubt in her eyes said it all.

"I don't trust anyone in Kane's orbit," she said finally, her voice low but steady. "Reed is playing his own game. We just have to make sure we stay one step ahead."

Alex sighed, running a hand through his hair. "He could turn on us at any moment."

Lena nodded, her face grim. "That's why we need to be ready. If Reed gives us the information we need, we use it. But if he tries to screw us, we take him down."

Alex's stomach tightened at her words. The idea of going up against Reed was terrifying enough. Going up against Reed *and* Kane? That felt like a death sentence.

"What exactly did he tell you?" Alex asked, his voice filled with tension. He had been too focused on Reed's demeanor during their meeting to absorb all the details of what the detective had said.

Lena walked over to the small table in the corner of the room, pulling out the crumpled piece of paper Reed had given her. She spread it out on the table, the dim light casting long shadows over the hastily scrawled notes.

"Reed's been keeping tabs on Kane's movements for months," Lena said, her eyes scanning the paper. "He knows where the real power lies—who Kane trusts, who holds the leverage in his operation."

Alex leaned in, his pulse quickening as he read over the notes. It was a detailed breakdown of Kane's inner circle—the people who kept his empire running. Political allies, business partners, enforcers. The names were all there, along with details about their roles and where they could be found.

"This is what we need," Lena continued, her voice hard. "If we can take out the key players in Kane's operation, the whole thing will collapse."

Alex's eyes darted over the list. He recognized some of the names—people they had heard about in whispers, shadowy figures who operated behind the scenes. But others were new, unknown. It was a web of power, and they were about to dismantle it piece by piece.

"There's more," Lena said, pulling another slip of paper from her jacket. This one was marked with a series of locations, coordinates scrawled in quick, precise handwriting. "Reed told me about a meeting Kane's having in three days. A private gathering with his most trusted allies."

Alex's heart skipped a beat. "You mean we could get all of them in one place?"

Lena nodded, her eyes gleaming with the intensity of the realization. "If we hit them there, we can take down the entire operation in one move."

It was a bold plan—almost too bold. But Alex could see the logic behind it. Kane's empire was vast, but it relied on a core group of people to keep the wheels turning. If they could take those people out, the rest would crumble.

But the risks were staggering.

"We'd be walking into the lion's den," Alex said, his voice thick with anxiety. "If anything goes wrong..."

Lena's eyes hardened. "We don't have another option. This is our chance. We hit them hard, and we take them all down."

The room fell silent again, the weight of the decision pressing down on both of them. Alex's mind raced with thoughts of what could go wrong, the dangers they were about to face. But deep down, he knew Lena was right. This was their best shot—their only shot.

He took a deep breath, his chest tight with fear and determination. "Then we need to prepare."

The next two days were a blur of preparation and tension. Alex and Lena worked around the clock, gathering what little resources they had left, planning every step of the operation with meticulous care. There was no room for error. If they were going to take down Kane's inner circle, they had to be precise.

Lena's contacts in the underground network came through with vital Intel on the location of the meeting—a secluded estate on the outskirts of the city, heavily guarded and isolated from the public eye. It was the perfect place for Kane to meet with his most trusted allies, and the perfect place for Alex and Lena to strike.

They had learned through Reed's notes that Kane's paranoia had grown since Alex and Lena's raid on his facility. Security had been tightened, and he had started isolating himself even more, trusting only a handful of people. The meeting was a gathering of those few, the people Kane relied on to keep his empire running.

"We have a small window," Lena said, studying the blueprints of the estate they had managed to obtain through their underground contacts. "They'll be vulnerable when they arrive, but once they're inside, it'll be locked down."

Alex stared at the blueprints, his mind racing with the possibilities. The estate was massive, surrounded by high walls and a dense forest. Security would be tight, with patrols stationed around the perimeter and cameras monitoring every entrance.

"We can't go in guns blazing," Lena continued, her voice sharp with focus. "We need to hit them before they have a chance to react."

Alex nodded, though the anxiety in his chest was growing with every passing second. This was more dangerous than anything they'd attempted before, and the stakes were higher than ever. But he knew they didn't have a choice. They had to go through with it.

"What about Reed?" Alex asked, glancing at Lena. "Do we trust him to hold up his end of the deal?"

Lena's expression darkened. "We don't have a choice. He's our way in."

The idea of relying on Reed still made Alex's skin crawl, but Lena was right. Without Reed's information, they wouldn't even know about the meeting. And without Reed's help, getting inside the estate would be nearly impossible.

"He'll be at the meeting too," Lena said, her voice quiet but filled with intensity. "Kane trusts him. But if he betrays us…"

Her words trailed off, but Alex understood the unspoken threat. If Reed turned on them, they wouldn't hesitate to take him out. This was war now, and there was no room for hesitation.

On the night of the operation, the tension between Alex and Lena was thick, almost suffocating. They had gone over the plan a dozen times, but the fear of the unknown still gnawed at them both. The risk of walking into a trap was real—Kane was no fool, and he had been playing this game far longer than they had.

The ride to the estate was silent, the car's engine the only sound breaking the stillness of the night. Alex stared out the window, his heart pounding in his chest as they approached the outskirts of the city. The weight of what they were about to do pressed down on him like a heavy shroud, but he forced himself to focus.

Lena was calm beside him, her hands steady on the wheel, but Alex could see the tension in her eyes. This mission was dangerous, and they both knew that not everyone would make it out alive. But Lena had always been the driving force behind their fight, the one who kept them going when things seemed impossible.

"We'll be in and out before they even realize what's happening," Lena said quietly, more to herself than to Alex. "We have to be."

Alex nodded, though his throat was tight with fear. They had planned for everything, but he knew that plans never survived first contact with the enemy. The only thing they could rely on now was each other—and whatever slim chance they had of turning the tide.

As they neared the estate, Lena pulled the car off the main road, parking in a secluded spot just beyond the tree line. They would have to make their way on foot from here, staying out of sight until they reached the perimeter.

Alex's heart pounded in his ears as they stepped out of the car, the cold night air biting at his skin. He checked his gear, his hands trembling slightly with the adrenaline coursing through his veins. This was it. The moment they had been working toward for so long.

Lena led the way through the trees, her movements quick and precise. Alex followed closely behind, his breath coming in shallow bursts as they approached the estate. The walls loomed ahead of them, tall and imposing, but there was no turning back now.

They reached the perimeter, crouching low behind a cluster of bushes as Lena scanned the area. The guards were exactly where Reed had said they would be—two stationed at the front gate, with another pair patrolling the perimeter. They moved in a predictable pattern, giving Lena and Alex the window they needed to slip inside.

"Ready?" Lena whispered, her eyes locking onto Alex's.

Alex nodded, his heart racing.

"Let's end this."

Chapter 31

Walking Into the Trap

The cold night pressed in around them as Alex and Lena crouched behind the wall of Kane's sprawling estate, the distant hum of voices and the clinking of glasses drifting from the mansion's grand interior. The towering structure loomed above them, a fortress of power and wealth, its sprawling lawns and high walls designed to keep people out—or trap them in.

The stakes had never been higher. Inside, Marcus Kane and his most trusted allies were gathering for a meeting that could decide the fate of the city—and Alex and Lena were about to crash the party. If they succeeded, Kane's empire would crumble. If they failed, it would be their end.

"This is it," Lena whispered, her breath visible in the cold night air. "Once we're inside, there's no turning back."

Alex nodded, his heart pounding in his chest. He glanced at Lena, her face illuminated by the faint moonlight filtering through the trees. She was calm, her eyes focused and determined, but he could sense the tension beneath her steely exterior. They had come too far, lost too much, to falter now.

"Are you ready?" Lena asked, her voice low and urgent.

Alex swallowed hard, feeling the weight of the gun tucked into his jacket. "As ready as I'll ever be."

Lena gave him a sharp nod, then motioned for him to follow her. They moved quickly and quietly across the dark lawn, staying low as they approached the side entrance Reed had told them about. The small, hidden door at the base of the wall was barely noticeable, but it was their way in.

Lena knelt in front of the door, her hands working swiftly to pick the lock. Alex kept watch, his pulse racing, every sound amplified in the tense silence. He could feel the weight of the estate pressing down on them, the looming presence of Kane and his men inside. They were walking into enemy territory, and every instinct in Alex's body was screaming at him to turn back.

But there was no turning back.

With a soft click, the lock disengaged, and Lena pushed the door open. They slipped inside, moving silently through the narrow tunnel that led to the heart of the estate. The air was cold and damp, the walls lined with pipes and electrical wiring that buzzed faintly in the dark. The tunnel stretched on for what felt like miles, winding deeper into the belly of Kane's empire.

"This leads to the lower levels," Lena whispered as they moved. "Once we're inside, we hit the surveillance room first. We can't let them see us coming."

Alex nodded, though his heart was racing. Every step felt like a descent into the unknown, and the weight of the danger ahead pressed down on him like a heavy shroud. But he had to stay focused. They had planned for this. They had gone over the details a hundred times. But still, the anxiety gnawed at him, a constant reminder that one wrong move could end everything.

They reached the end of the tunnel, emerging into a small storage room filled with crates and equipment. The estate's grandeur was hidden behind layers of concrete and steel, but Alex knew that just above them, Kane and his allies were gathered in luxury, unaware of the storm about to hit them.

Lena motioned for Alex to follow her as she led the way through the maze of corridors. The estate was massive, a sprawling labyrinth of hallways and rooms, but Lena knew exactly where they were going. Reed's Intel had been precise, and for now, they had to trust that he hadn't set them up.

The surveillance room was on the second floor, hidden behind layers of security, but Lena made quick work of the locks and access codes. They moved through the darkened hallways, their steps silent, their movements swift. Every corner they turned, every door they opened brought them closer to the moment of truth.

When they finally reached the surveillance room, Lena wasted no time disabling the cameras. She moved with precision, her fingers flying across the console as the monitors blinked off, one by one. Alex stood guard by the door, his heart pounding in his chest as he watched the hallway for any signs of movement.

"All clear," Lena whispered, stepping away from the console. "They won't see us coming."

Alex let out a breath he hadn't realized he'd been holding. The tension between them was thick, the weight of what they were about to do pressing down on them with every breath. They had the element of surprise now, but that wouldn't last. They had to move fast.

"Let's go," Lena said, her voice tight with determination. "We need to hit them before they have a chance to react."

They moved quickly through the upper levels of the estate, sticking to the shadows as they made their way toward the private conference room where Kane and his inner circle were meeting. The tension between them was palpable, the air thick with the anticipation of what was about to unfold.

Alex's heart raced as they approached the large wooden doors that led into the conference room. His mind was filled with images of the men they were about to face—the most powerful and dangerous individuals in the city, all gathered in one place. If they succeeded, Kane's empire would crumble. If they failed, they wouldn't make it out alive.

"This is it," Lena whispered, her voice barely audible. "Are you ready?"

Alex swallowed hard, nodding. "Let's finish this."

Lena gave him a brief nod, then reached for the door. With a soft push, the door swung open, revealing the room beyond.

The scene inside was a stark contrast to the tension outside. The men around the table were dressed in expensive suits, sipping whiskey from crystal glasses, their laughter and quiet conversation filling the air. They didn't notice Alex and Lena at first, too absorbed in their own world of power and influence.

And there, at the head of the table, sat **Marcus Kane**.

The sight of him sent a chill down Alex's spine. Kane was everything Alex had imagined—tall, imposing, his presence filling the room with a dark energy that made the air feel heavy. His eyes, cold and calculating, flicked up to meet Alex's as he stepped into the room.

A moment of silence fell over the room, the laughter and conversation dying instantly as Kane's gaze moved between Alex and Lena. The men around the table stiffened, their eyes narrowing with suspicion. They hadn't expected this. They hadn't expected to be confronted, here in their fortress of power.

"So," Kane said, his voice low and smooth, "you finally decided to show yourselves."

Lena's face was hard, her hand resting on the gun at her side. "It's over, Kane. We have everything. The files, the proof. Your empire is finished."

Kane's lips curled into a small, humourless smile. He didn't stand, didn't flinch. He simply looked at them, his eyes gleaming with cold amusement. "Is that what you think?"

Before Alex could react, Kane pressed a button under the table, and the doors behind them slammed shut with a loud thud. The sound of heavy footsteps echoed from the hallways outside, growing louder by the second. They were surrounded.

Alex's heart raced as the realization hit him—they had walked into a trap.

Kane stood slowly, his movements deliberate, his eyes never leaving Lena's. "You've been a thorn in my side for too long," he said, his voice like a dark whisper. "But it's over now."

The doors on either side of the room burst open, and a flood of armed guards poured in, their guns raised, their faces cold and expressionless. They moved with military precision, forming a wall around Alex and Lena, cutting off any chance of escape.

The men around the table stood as well, their faces hardening as they reached for their weapons. The room was suddenly charged with danger, the air thick with the threat of violence.

Lena's hand shot to her gun, her eyes darting around the room as she assessed the situation. They were outnumbered, outgunned, and cornered.

Kane stepped forward, his eyes gleaming with satisfaction. "You should have known better than to come here. But I have to admit, your little game has been entertaining."

Alex's pulse pounded in his ears, his mind racing as he tried to think of a way out. The guards were closing in, their weapons trained on them, and there was no way they could fight their way through. They were trapped.

But Lena wasn't done fighting.

With lightning speed, she drew her gun, firing off a series of precise shots. The first guard dropped before he had a chance to react, his body crumpling to the floor. The room erupted into chaos.

"Move!" Lena shouted, her voice sharp with urgency.

Alex didn't hesitate. He dove behind the table, his heart pounding in his chest as bullets ricocheted off the walls around him. The men at the table scattered, ducking for cover as Lena continued to fire, taking down one guard after another with deadly precision.

But there were too many of them.

Kane's guards were highly trained, moving with ruthless efficiency as they closed in on Alex and Lena. The room filled with the deafening sound of gunfire, the air thick with smoke and adrenaline.

Alex fired his gun, his hands shaking as he tried to hit his targets. His shots were wild, unfocused, but he managed to take down one of the guards. He ducked behind the heavy oak table, his breath coming in ragged gasps as he tried to catch his bearings.

"Alex, the window!" Lena shouted, her voice cutting through the chaos.

Alex's eyes darted to the far end of the room, where a small, narrow window stood as their only chance of escape. It was their only way out.

"We need to get to the window!" Lena yelled, firing another shot at the advancing guards.

Alex's pulse raced as he scrambled to his feet, his heart pounding in his chest. The guards were closing in, their movements quick and deadly. If they didn't move now, they would be overwhelmed.

Lena fired one last shot, then grabbed Alex's arm, pulling him toward the window. They sprinted across the room, dodging bullets as they went, the sound of gunfire deafening in their ears.

They reached the window, but it was too high to climb through.

"Boost me up!" Lena shouted, her voice tight with strain.

Alex nodded, his heart racing as he crouched down, bracing himself as Lena stepped onto his hands. He pushed her up, his arms trembling with the effort as she grabbed the ledge and hoisted herself through the narrow opening.

"Hurry!" Lena yelled from the other side.

Alex's chest tightened as he glanced back at the room. The guards were closing in, their guns raised, their eyes cold and calculating.

There was no time.

With one final burst of adrenaline, Alex pulled himself up, squeezing through the narrow window just as a bullet grazed his arm. He grunted in pain but forced himself to keep moving, his body trembling as he hit the ground on the other side.

Lena grabbed his arm, pulling him to his feet. "Come on! We're not out yet!"

They sprinted into the night, the sound of gunfire and shouting fading behind them as they disappeared into the shadows of the estate's vast grounds. The cold air bit at their skin, but Alex barely felt it. His mind was racing, his pulse pounding as they ran through the trees, their footsteps muffled by the soft earth beneath them.

But they weren't safe yet.

Kane's men would be after them soon, and the clock was ticking.

Chapter 32

The Chase

The cold air bit at Alex's skin as he and Lena sprinted through the dense trees surrounding Kane's estate, their footsteps muffled by the wet earth beneath them. The sounds of gunfire and shouting faded into the distance, but Alex knew better than to believe they were safe. The estate was a fortress, and Kane's men would already be on their trail, hunting them through the forest like prey.

His chest burned with the effort of running, his breath coming in sharp, ragged gasps, but he couldn't slow down. Every muscle in his body screamed for rest, but he pushed through the pain. There was no stopping now—not when they were so close to being caught.

Lena was just ahead of him, her pace quick and unrelenting. She hadn't spoken since they'd escaped through the window, her face set in hard lines, her focus entirely on getting them as far away from Kane's men as possible. Her movements were fluid, precise, her body working on instinct as they wove through the thick underbrush.

Alex's heart pounded in his chest, a frantic rhythm that matched the thudding of his boots against the earth. His mind raced with the events of the last hour—Kane's cold smile, the trap they had walked into, the chaos of the gunfight. They had come so close to losing everything, and now they were being hunted. Kane had set them up, and they had barely escaped with their lives.

His arm throbbed where the bullet had grazed him, but he couldn't afford to stop and tend to it. Not now. Not with Kane's men so close behind.

"Faster," Lena urged, her voice barely audible over the sound of their breathing. "We need to put more distance between us and the estate."

Alex nodded, though his body was screaming in protest. His legs felt like lead, every step heavier than the last, but he pushed forward, following Lena deeper into the woods. The thick canopy of trees provided some cover, but it also disoriented him. Everything looked the same—twisted branches, thick underbrush, patches of darkness where the moonlight couldn't reach.

Lena had said there was a clearing somewhere ahead, where they could regroup and figure out their next move. But with every passing second, Alex felt the pressure mounting. They were running out of time.

"How long do you think before they catch up?" Alex asked between gasps of air.

Lena didn't slow her pace, her eyes scanning the shadows ahead. "Not long. They'll have dogs and helicopters soon if they haven't already. Kane doesn't take chances."

Alex's stomach twisted at the thought. He could already hear the faint thrum of engines in the distance, growing louder with every passing moment. Kane's reach was vast, and he had resources far beyond what Alex and Lena could match. They were running out of places to hide, and Kane wouldn't stop until they were dead.

"We need a plan," Alex said, his voice tight with fear and exhaustion.

Lena shot him a quick glance, her expression unreadable. "I know."

They pushed on, their pace relentless as the sound of helicopters grew louder, cutting through the quiet of the forest like a warning bell. The whir of the rotors sent a chill down Alex's spine, and he glanced up at the night sky, searching for the dark shapes of the helicopters above the treetops.

"We need to get out of the open," Lena said, her voice low but urgent. "They'll have thermal imaging. We're exposed here."

Alex's pulse quickened, the weight of her words pressing down on him. He knew what that meant—no matter how fast they ran, Kane's men would find them. The helicopters would scan the forest, their thermal cameras picking up on the heat signatures of their bodies, tracking their every move. They were being hunted.

"What do we do?" Alex asked, his voice laced with panic.

Lena's eyes flicked to the tree line ahead. "There's a river about a mile north of here. We get to it, use the water to mask our heat signatures."

It wasn't much of a plan, but it was the best option they had. The river would buy them time, give them a chance to slip away from the thermal cameras. But the distance between them and the river felt impossibly long. Alex's legs burned with the effort of running, and he could feel the exhaustion seeping into his bones. But he didn't have a choice. They had to keep moving.

"Let's go," Lena said, her pace quickening.

They veered north, cutting through the thick underbrush as the sound of helicopters grew louder overhead. Alex's heart pounded in his chest, his breath coming in shallow gasps as they sprinted through the trees. He could feel the pressure mounting, the weight of Kane's men closing in around them like a vice.

The roar of the river reached Alex's ears before he saw it, a rushing torrent of water cutting through the forest like a lifeline. The sight of it filled him with a surge of hope, but it was quickly tempered by the realization that they were still being hunted. The sound of helicopters thundering overhead grew louder, the beams of searchlights slicing through the trees, sweeping the ground for any sign of movement.

"We have to move fast," Lena said, her voice tight with urgency. "The water will mask us, but they'll know we're heading for it."

Alex nodded, his heart racing as they reached the riverbank. The water rushed by in a chaotic swirl of dark currents, its surface glittering faintly in the moonlight. It was deeper than he had expected, the current strong enough to pull them under if they weren't careful.

"We'll follow the river downstream," Lena said, scanning the surrounding forest for any sign of pursuit. "Stay close to the bank, but don't get out until we're far enough away."

Alex swallowed hard, his pulse quickening as he waded into the freezing water. The cold hit him like a shock, stealing his breath and sending a shudder through his body. But there was no time to hesitate. They had to keep moving.

The water rose quickly, reaching Alex's waist as he followed Lena into the river. The current was stronger than he had anticipated, pulling at his legs with every step, but Lena moved with purpose, her eyes focused ahead as she guided them downstream.

The helicopters passed overhead, their searchlights cutting through the trees, but the river offered some protection. The sound of the rushing water drowned out the roar of the engines, and the thick canopy of trees overhead provided cover from the thermal cameras.

For a moment, Alex allowed himself to believe they might actually escape.

But the river was treacherous, the current pulling at them with increasing force. Every step was a struggle, the cold water sapping their strength and making it harder to move. Alex's muscles burned with the effort, his body trembling from the cold, but he forced himself to keep going.

"We're almost there," Lena said, her voice barely audible over the roar of the water.

Alex nodded, though his body felt like it was on the verge of collapse. His legs were numb, his breath coming in shallow, painful gasps, but he kept moving, following Lena downstream. The forest around them seemed to close in, the thick trees casting long shadows over the river, but they were getting farther from the estate. With every step, the sounds of helicopters grew fainter, the searchlights no longer visible through the canopy.

"We can get out here," Lena said, motioning toward a small, rocky bank up ahead. "We've put enough distance between us and the estate."

Alex followed her toward the bank, his body shaking with exhaustion as they pulled themselves out of the freezing water. The cold air hit him like a wall, but the adrenaline coursing through his veins kept him moving.

They collapsed onto the rocky shore, gasping for breath. The cold seeped into Alex's bones, but for the first time in hours, the pressure eased just slightly. They had made it—for now.

Lena was already on her feet, her eyes scanning the surrounding forest. "We need to keep moving," she said, her voice tight with urgency. "Kane's men won't stop just because we got to the river. They'll keep coming."

Alex nodded, though his body ached with the need to rest. They couldn't afford to stop. Not yet. Kane's reach was vast, and he wouldn't let them go that easily.

They moved through the dense forest in silence, the sounds of the river fading behind them. The adrenaline that had carried Alex through the river crossing was beginning to wear off, leaving behind a deep exhaustion that weighed down every step. His muscles screamed in protest, his breath coming in ragged gasps, but he pushed forward, driven by the knowledge that stopping meant death.

Lena led the way, her face set in hard lines, her movements deliberate. She hadn't spoken since they left the river, her focus entirely on getting them as far from Kane's men as possible. Alex could see the strain on her face, the exhaustion that mirrored his own, but Lena was relentless. She wouldn't stop until they were safe.

But as they moved deeper into the forest, the weight of the situation pressed down on Alex like a heavy shroud. They were running, constantly running, but where could they go? Kane's reach extended far beyond the estate, and even if they managed to evade his men tonight, he would keep coming for them. He always had more resources, more allies, more ways to hunt them down.

"We can't keep running forever," Alex said, his voice low and filled with frustration.

Lena glanced at him, her expression hardening. "I know. But we don't have a choice right now."

Alex's chest tightened with the weight of her words. She was right—there was no time for second-guessing, no time to dwell on their dwindling options. But the constant pressure, the relentless chase, was wearing him down. The fear of being caught, the exhaustion of constantly being on the move—it was all starting to take its toll.

"We have to find a way to end this," Alex said, his voice breaking slightly. "We can't keep doing this."

Lena stopped suddenly, turning to face him. Her eyes were filled with a mixture of determination and something darker—something raw and unresolved. "We *will* end this," she said, her voice sharp. "But we need to stay alive first."

Alex's heart pounded in his chest as he met her gaze. The intensity in her eyes was undeniable, but beneath it, he could see the toll this was taking on her too. She was just as tired, just as scared, but she wouldn't let herself break. She couldn't afford to.

"I'm not giving up," Lena said, her voice quieter now, though no less resolute. "We've come too far. We've lost too much. But I need you with me, Alex. I can't do this alone."

Her words hit him like a punch to the gut. He had known Lena for so long, trusted her through everything, but hearing the vulnerability in her voice, the admission that she needed him, struck a chord deep inside him. They were both carrying the weight of this fight, but they were still human—still fragile beneath the armour they had built around themselves.

"I'm with you," Alex said, his voice steady despite the storm raging inside him. "Always."

Lena nodded, her eyes softening just slightly. "Good. Because we're not done yet."

They pushed deeper into the forest, their pace slowing as the adrenaline continued to fade. The night stretched on, cold and unforgiving, but they kept moving, driven by the knowledge that Kane's men were still out there, hunting them.

But as they walked, a plan began to form in Alex's mind. They couldn't keep running, but they could use Kane's relentless pursuit against him. They had to turn the tables—find a way to strike back before he could tighten the noose around them.

"We need to hit Kane where it hurts," Alex said after a long stretch of silence. "We can't outrun him forever, but if we can find his weak spot…"

Lena glanced at him, her eyes narrowing. "What are you thinking?"

"Kane's empire is built on power, control, and fear," Alex said, his mind racing. "We need to take that away from him. If we can expose him, show the world what he's really doing—"

"He'll lose everything," Lena finished, her voice sharp with understanding. "But we need proof. More than we already have."

Alex nodded. "We need to find out who else is tied to him, who's protecting him, and bring it all down. Reed's information is a start, but we need more."

Lena's eyes gleamed with determination. "Then we go after his network. We find the people he's been using to stay untouchable."

It was a dangerous plan—one that would require going deeper into Kane's world than they ever had before. But it was their only chance. If they could dismantle the web of corruption and power that Kane had woven, they could bring him down once and for all.

"We can't do it alone," Alex said, his voice steady but filled with uncertainty. "We'll need help."

Lena nodded, her jaw tight with resolve. "Then we find allies. People who want to see Kane fall as much as we do."

They had a new goal now, a way to fight back instead of just surviving. But the road ahead was long and filled with danger. Kane's empire was vast, and every step they took toward dismantling it would bring them closer to the edge.

But Alex and Lena had made it this far. They weren't about to give up now.

"We'll take him down," Alex said, his voice filled with quiet determination. "Piece by piece."

Lena's eyes locked onto his, a fierce light burning behind them. "Then let's finish this."

Chapter 33

Striking Back

The moon had long since vanished behind thick clouds, leaving the forest in a heavy, impenetrable darkness. Alex and Lena moved swiftly but quietly, their steps muted by the dense underbrush. The silence between them was thick with unspoken tension, but there was also a shared understanding—they had crossed a line. They were no longer just running; they were preparing for war.

After hours of trekking through the wilderness, they finally reached the edge of the city. It was strange, seeing the towering skyline after what felt like a lifetime spent in the shadows of Kane's empire. But they couldn't afford to linger. Kane's men were still out there, and they needed to move fast.

Lena glanced at Alex, her face illuminated by the faint glow of the streetlights in the distance. "We need to reach Elena," she said, her voice steady but urgent. "She's our best shot at finding the allies we need."

Alex nodded, his mind racing with the plan they had pieced together during their long walk. Elena Vasquez had connections in the underground—journalists, whistleblowers, people who had been quietly fighting against Kane for years. But they had always operated in the shadows, too afraid to challenge Kane directly. Now, Alex and Lena needed them to step into the light.

"We have to convince them that we can win," Alex said, his voice low. "If they think we're just going to get ourselves killed, they won't help."

Lena's jaw clenched, but she nodded. "We'll make them see. We've got enough dirt on Kane to expose him. We just need the right people to help us get it out."

The city seemed quieter than usual as they made their way through the narrow streets, staying close to the shadows. It was late, and the usual hum of traffic and voices was muted, replaced by the distant sound of sirens and the occasional flicker of headlights from passing cars. Kane's men were still out there, searching for them, but they had the advantage of knowing the city's back alleys and hidden corners.

When they finally reached Elena's safe house, a rundown apartment building on the outskirts of the city, Alex felt a flicker of hope. The building was unassuming, its windows dark and boarded up, but it was one of the few places in the city where they could hide for a while.

Lena knocked softly on the door, her eyes scanning the street for any signs of trouble. The door opened a crack, and Elena's sharp eyes peered out from behind the heavy chain.

"About time," Elena muttered, unlocking the door and motioning for them to come inside. "I've been listening to police scanners all night. You two are causing quite a stir."

"We don't have much time," Lena said, her voice tense as she stepped inside. "Kane's men are still hunting us, but we need your help."

Elena shut the door behind them, locking it with a series of deadbolts. She turned to face them, her expression hard but curious. "I figured you'd be asking for a favour. What exactly do you need?"

Alex stepped forward, his heart pounding in his chest. "We need allies. People who can help us expose Kane, take him down for good."

Elena raised an eyebrow. "You've got proof?"

Lena pulled the files from her bag, spreading them out on the small, rickety table in the center of the room. "We've got everything—financial records, blackmail material, documents linking Kane to every corrupt politician and business leader in the city. But it's not enough. We need people who can take this public, people who won't get scared off or bought out."

Elena's sharp eyes scanned the files, her expression unreadable. After a long moment, she looked up at them, her lips curling into a thin smile. "You've got guts, I'll give you that. But Kane's been untouchable for years. What makes you think you can take him down now?"

"Because we're not just going after him," Alex said, his voice filled with quiet determination. "We're going after his entire network. The people who prop him up, who protect him. We expose them, and the whole thing collapses."

Elena leaned back in her chair, crossing her arms over her chest. "And you think you can find people willing to risk their lives for this?"

"We know you have contacts," Lena said, her voice sharp. "People who've been waiting for a chance to fight back."

Elena studied them for a long moment, her eyes narrowing as she considered their words. Finally, she nodded. "I can reach out to a few people.

Journalists, activists, some whistleblowers who've been looking for an opportunity to bring Kane down. But it's going to take more than a few names on a piece of paper to convince them."

Lena glanced at Alex, her eyes filled with determination. "Then we give them more. We make it clear that this is their only chance."

Elena smiled, though there was no warmth in it. "You're playing a dangerous game, but I like it. Give me a few hours. I'll see what I can do."

The next few hours passed in a blur of tense anticipation. While Elena reached out to her contacts, Alex and Lena poured over the files, piecing together the full extent of Kane's empire. The corruption ran deep—politicians, law enforcement, business magnates—all tied to Kane's sprawling network of influence. It was a web of deceit and power that had kept him untouchable for years.

But now, they had a way to unravel it.

"This is the key," Lena said, her voice filled with quiet intensity as she pointed to a series of documents linking Kane to a high-ranking official. "This man—Senator Martin—is the lynchpin. He's been protecting Kane from the inside, keeping the authorities off his back."

Alex's heart raced as he studied the documents. "If we expose him, Kane will lose his protection. The police, the feds—they'll have no choice but to go after him."

Lena nodded, her eyes gleaming with determination. "But we need to get this to the right people. If we leak it to the wrong outlet, Kane's people will bury it before it ever sees the light of day."

"That's where Elena's contacts come in," Alex said, his mind racing with the possibilities. "We need someone who can get this out to the public—someone who can't be bought."

As they worked, Alex couldn't shake the feeling of dread that hung over him. They were closer than ever to bringing Kane down, but the danger was growing with every step they took. Kane wasn't a man who took betrayal lightly, and if he found out what they were planning, he would come for them with everything he had.

"We can do this," Lena said, her voice breaking through his thoughts. "We've come too far to back down now."

Alex nodded, though the fear gnawed at him. They were walking a tightrope, and one misstep could send them plummeting.

A knock at the door jolted them both out of their thoughts. Elena stepped into the room, her face set in hard lines.

"I've got people willing to help," she said, her voice low but firm. "But they want to meet. They want to know what they're risking their lives for."

Lena glanced at Alex, her expression filled with steely resolve. "Then let's show them."

The meeting was held in the basement of an old, abandoned factory on the outskirts of the city. The building had long since fallen into disrepair, its windows shattered, the walls covered in graffiti. It was the perfect place for a secret gathering—far from Kane's watchful eyes.

As Alex and Lena entered the dimly lit room, they were met by a group of men and women, their faces tense but determined. These were the people Elena had brought together—journalists, whistleblowers, activists, and even a few former law enforcement officers. They were the ones who had been quietly fighting against Kane's influence for years, but now they were ready to take a stand.

Lena wasted no time. She laid the files out on the table, her voice steady as she explained their plan.

"Kane has been running this city for too long," she said, her voice echoing in the quiet room. "He's bought off politicians, law enforcement, and the media. But we have the proof. We can expose him, take down his entire network."

One of the journalists, a grizzled man with a hardened expression, leaned forward. "And what's stopping Kane from silencing us before we can get this out?"

Alex stepped in, his voice filled with urgency. "That's why we need to hit him fast. Once we release this, we go public immediately. Kane's people won't be able to cover it up if the entire city is watching."

Another woman, an activist with fiery eyes, nodded. "He's too powerful. But if we can break his hold on the media, we can get the truth out."

Elena crossed her arms, her eyes scanning the room. "We have to move quickly. Kane's already hunting Alex and Lena. It's only a matter of time before he finds out what we're planning."

The room fell silent as everyone considered the weight of Elena's words. The danger was real. Kane wouldn't hesitate to kill anyone who threatened his empire. But Alex could see the determination in their faces. They were tired of living in fear.

"We do this together," Lena said, her voice strong. "We expose Kane, and we take back this city."

For a long moment, no one spoke. Then, one by one, the people around the table nodded, their faces set with resolve.

"We're in," the journalist said, his voice low but firm. "Let's take him down."

With their allies gathered, Alex and Lena began to prepare for the final strike. They worked through the night, coordinating with the journalists and activists to ensure that the evidence would be released simultaneously across multiple platforms—social media, independent news outlets, even major networks that couldn't afford to ignore the story once it broke.

As the hours ticked by, the tension between them grew. They were on the verge of bringing down one of the most powerful men in the city, but they were also walking into the lion's den. Kane wouldn't go down without a fight.

"We need to be ready for anything," Lena said, her voice low as they stood outside the factory, the cold night air biting at their skin. "Once this goes live, Kane will come for us. And he'll come hard."

Alex nodded, his stomach tight with fear and anticipation. "We'll be ready."

They had been running for so long, constantly looking over their shoulders, always one step ahead of Kane's men. But now, they were ready to stop running. They were ready to fight.

As dawn broke over the city, the final preparations were made. The evidence was uploaded, the networks were primed, and their allies were in place. All that was left was to pull the trigger.

Lena glanced at Alex, her eyes filled with a mixture of fear and determination. "This is it."

Alex's heart pounded in his chest, but he forced himself to nod. "Let's end this."

With a single press of a button, the files went live.

Epilogue

A Fragile Peace

A Moment of Calm

The salty breeze off the ocean was warm, gentle, and soothing—everything Alex needed after the storm that had consumed his life for the past few months. The blue horizon stretched out endlessly before him, the rhythmic crash of waves against the shore a welcome relief from the constant noise of the city, the gunfire, the tension of being hunted. For the first time in what felt like forever, Alex could breathe.

He sat back in his chair, gazing out at the pristine beach. The tropical island was a paradise, untouched by the corruption and chaos he had left behind. It was the vacation he had promised himself once Kane was taken down, though part of him hadn't believed he'd survive long enough to enjoy it.

Lena was still in the city, helping tie up the last loose ends of their operation against Kane's network. She had insisted that Alex get away, clear his head, and find some semblance of peace after everything they'd been through. And for a while, it worked. The island was beautiful, secluded, far from the world of high-stakes danger and crime.

For a few days, Alex allowed himself to relax, to forget. But peace, it seemed, wasn't meant to last.

The salty breeze off the ocean was warm, gentle, and soothing—everything Alex needed after the storm that had consumed his life for the past few months. The blue horizon stretched out endlessly before him, the rhythmic crash of waves against the shore a welcome relief from the constant noise of the city, the gunfire, and the tension of being hunted. For the first time in what felt like forever, Alex could breathe.

He sat back in his chair, gazing out at the pristine beach. The tropical island was a paradise, untouched by the corruption and chaos he had left behind. It was the vacation he had promised himself once Kane was taken down, though part of him hadn't believed he'd survive long enough to enjoy it.

Lena was still in the city, helping tie up the last loose ends of their operation against Kane's network. She had insisted that Alex get away, clear his head, and find some semblance of peace after everything they'd been through. And for a while, it worked. The island was beautiful, secluded, far from the world of high-stakes danger and crime.

For a few days, Alex allowed himself to relax, to forget. But peace, it seemed, wasn't meant to last.

The Stranger at the Bar

It was on the fifth day of his vacation that Alex first noticed the man. He had been sitting in the beachfront bar, sipping a cold drink and watching the sunset, when the stranger entered. At first, Alex didn't think much of it—the man looked like any other tourist, dressed in casual beachwear, sunglasses perched atop his head. But something about him felt...off.

The man sat alone at the far end of the bar, his back to the ocean, his posture stiff and tense. Alex watched out of the corner of his eye as the man ordered a drink, his fingers drumming nervously on the countertop. There was a strange energy to him, like he was waiting for something—or someone.

Alex's instincts, honed by months of being hunted, were already on high alert. He tried to brush it off, reminding himself that he was supposed to be on vacation, but the nagging feeling in his gut wouldn't go away.

As the sun dipped lower on the horizon, casting the bar in a warm orange glow, the stranger's phone buzzed. He answered it quickly, his voice low and hurried, but in the quiet of the bar, Alex could hear enough to catch snippets of the conversation.

"No...not yet. I'm still waiting... Yes, it's all set, but the transfer hasn't gone through yet."

Alex stiffened, his mind immediately snapping into focus. He had heard conversations like this before—too many times, in fact. The words were vague, innocuous to an untrained ear, but to Alex, they were a red flag. Transfers. Waiting. It sounded like a deal, or worse—something criminal.

Alex tried to turn his attention back to his drink, but his mind was racing. His vacation was supposed to be an escape, a break from the dangerous world he had spent the past year fighting. But the more he thought about it, the more he realized that danger never truly went away. It only hid in plain sight.

The stranger finished his call and stood abruptly, throwing a few bills onto the bar before heading for the door. As he passed Alex, their eyes met for the briefest of moments—just long enough for Alex to catch the tension in the man's face, the anxiety behind his forced smile.

Alex watched as the man disappeared down the beach, his mind now buzzing with questions. He could ignore it, pretend it was nothing. He could continue with his vacation, enjoy the sun, and let the stranger's odd behaviour slip into the background.

But Alex had never been good at letting things go.